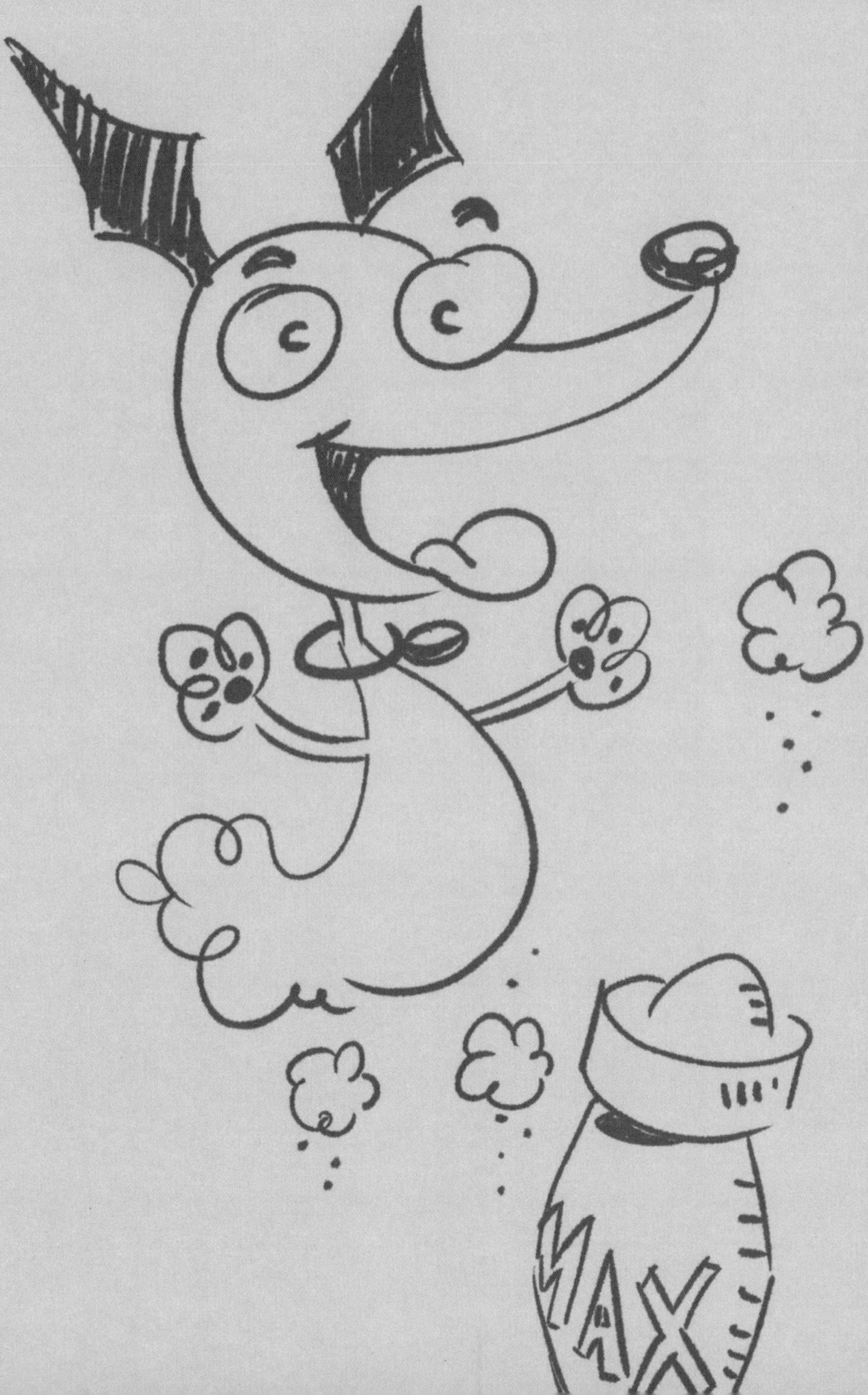

THE DEADENING

By Dana Sullivan

RED
CHAIR
·PRESS·

Dead Max Comix is produced and published by:
Red Chair Press   PO Box 333   South Egremont, MA 01258-0333
www.redchairpress.com

To my three great dogs, past and present, Mike, Max and Bennie,
and to all the dogs who bring unconditional love, joy, humor and
clogged vacuums to their lucky humans around the world.

Publisher's Cataloging-In-Publication Data
Names: Sullivan, Dana, 1958- author, illustrator.
Title: The deadening / by Dana Sullivan.

Description: South Egremont, MA : Red Chair Press, [2020] | Series: Dead
    Max comix ; book 1 | Interest age level: 009-013. | Summary: "Derrick
    Hollis is a 7th grader at Zachary Taylor Middle School and an aspiring
    cartoonist too shy to show his work to anybody but his best friend
    Doug. Derrick is devastated when his dog Max dies. But after being
    cremated, Max returns from the other side and starts giving Derrick
    advice. Derrick could use it, especially when it comes to affairs of
    the heart and standing up to bullies."--Provided by publisher.

Identifiers: ISBN 9781634408523 (library hardcover) | ISBN 9781634408530
    (paperback) | ISBN 9781634408547 (ebook PDF)

Subjects: LCSH: Middle school students--Comic books, strips, etc. | Dogs--
    Comic books, strips, etc. | Spirits--Comic books, strips, etc. |
    Bullying--Comic books, strips, etc. | CYAC: Middle school students--
    Cartoons and comics. | Dogs--Cartoons and comics. | Spirits--Cartoons
    and comics. | Bullying--Cartoons and comics. | LCGFT: Graphic novels.

Classification: LCC PZ7.7 .S85 2020 (print) | LCC PZ7.7 (ebook) | DDC
    741.5973 [Fic]--dc23

LC record available at https://lccn.loc.gov/2019931706

Text & Illustration copyright © 2020 Dana Sullivan
RED CHAIR PRESS, the RED CHAIR and associated logos are registered
trademarks of Red Chair Press LLC.

Printed in the United States of America

09 1P CGBS20

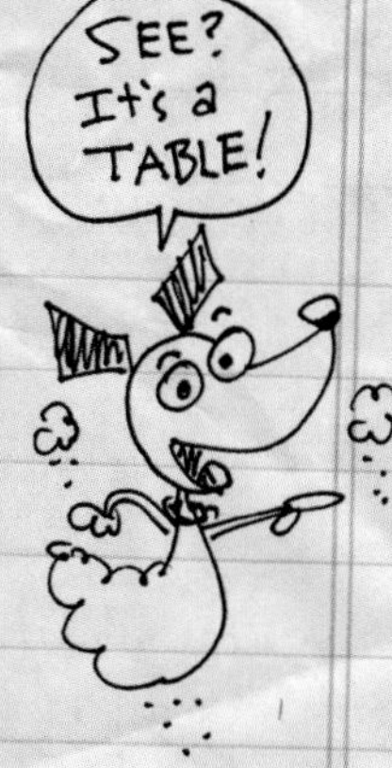
SEE? It's a TABLE!

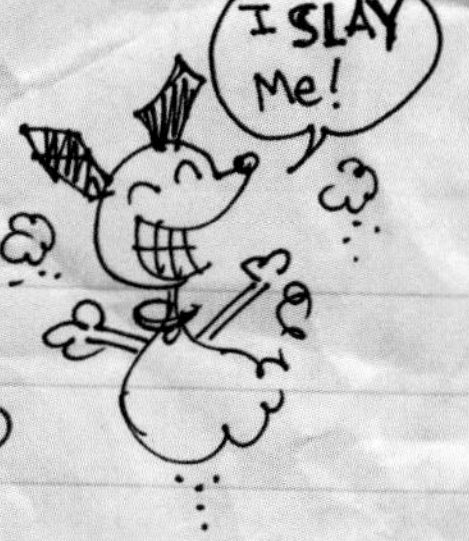
I SLAY Me!

Table of CONTENTS

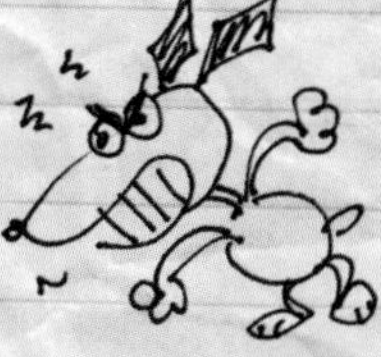

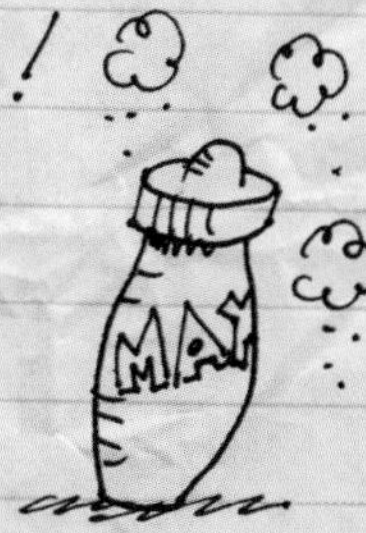
MAX

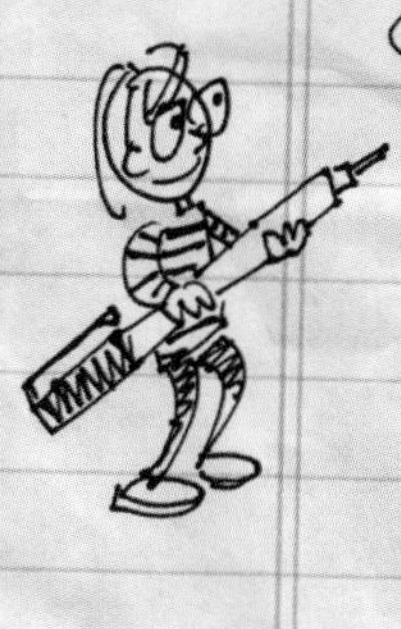

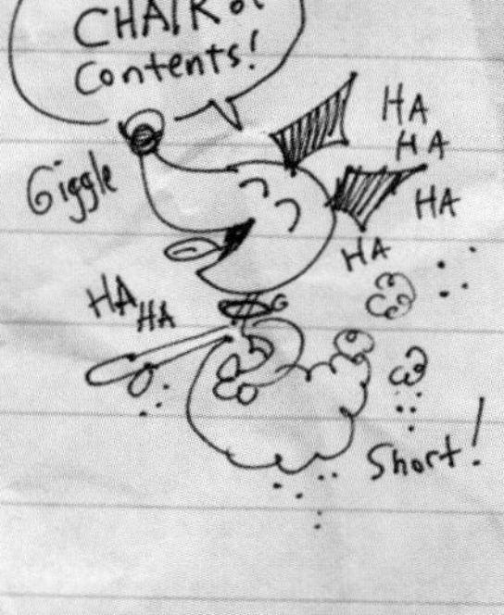
the CHAIR of Contents!
Giggle
HA HA HA
HA
HA HA
Short!

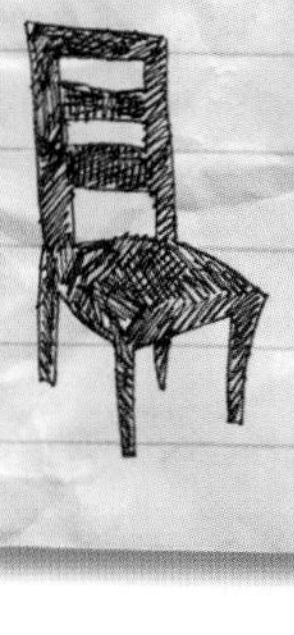

3RD Period · Mr. Newcomb
Derrick Hollis
GRAPHIC ARTS class
Due Monday: Sketches for GRAPHIC NOVEL
Plot, problem, challenges, solution, story arc,
ACTION!
Who are you?
Me STORY ORC!
Who You?
I'm Frito!
Mr. Newcomb
Nuke'em!
BOOM!
IDEAS: NukeMan, the Atomic Teacher ⇐ DANGER!
FLATMAN & RIBBON
this sucks!
Diary of a Shrimpy Kid
What about ME?
Revenge of the VOLE?
Did you say MOLE?
MAX the DOG?

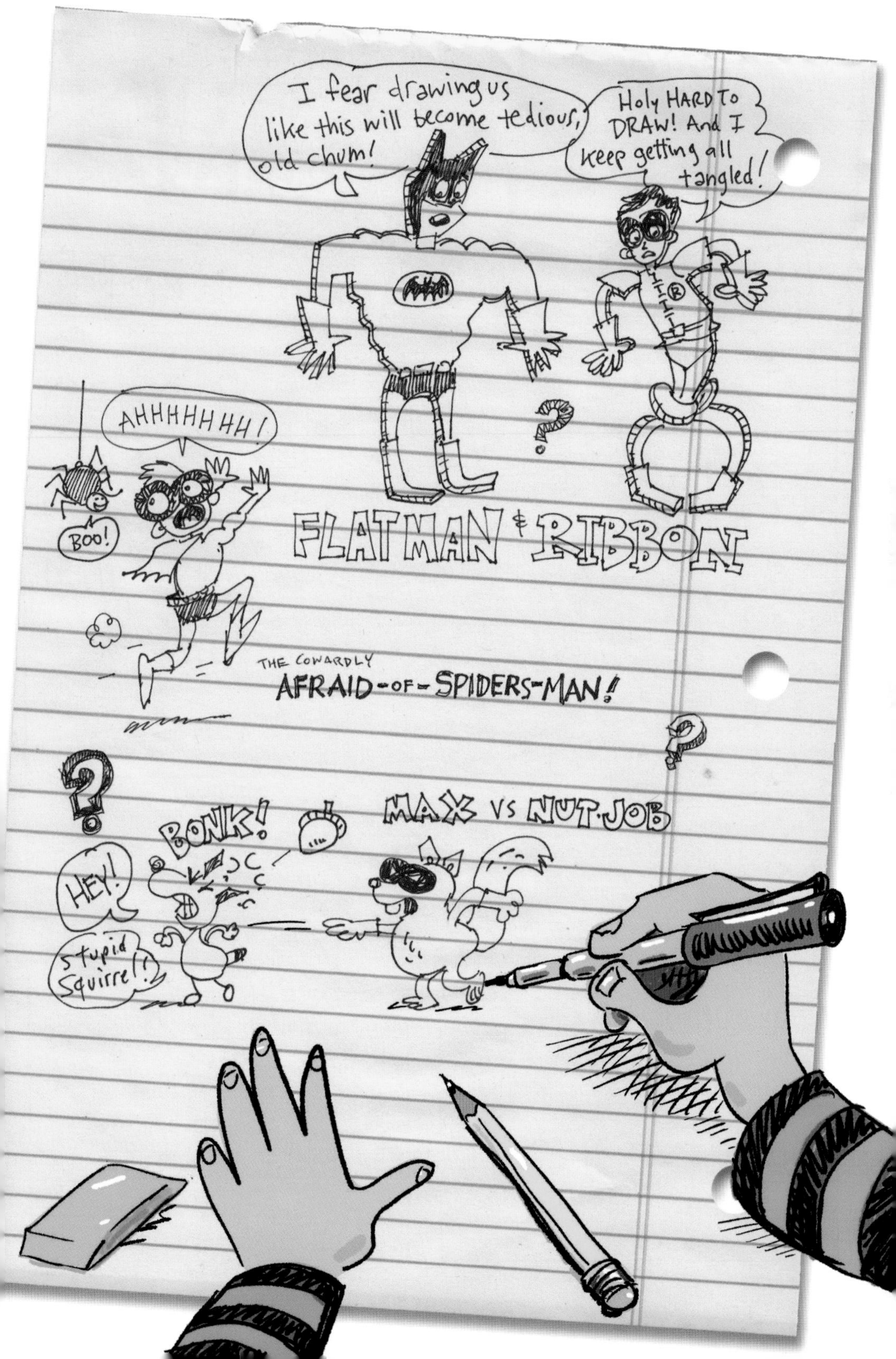
I fear drawing us like this will become tedious, old chum!
Holy HARD TO DRAW! And I keep getting all tangled!
AHHHHHHH!
BOO!
FLATMAN & RIBBON
THE COWARDLY AFRAID-OF-SPIDERS-MAN!
MAX VS NUT-JOB
BONK!
HEY!
stupid squirrel!

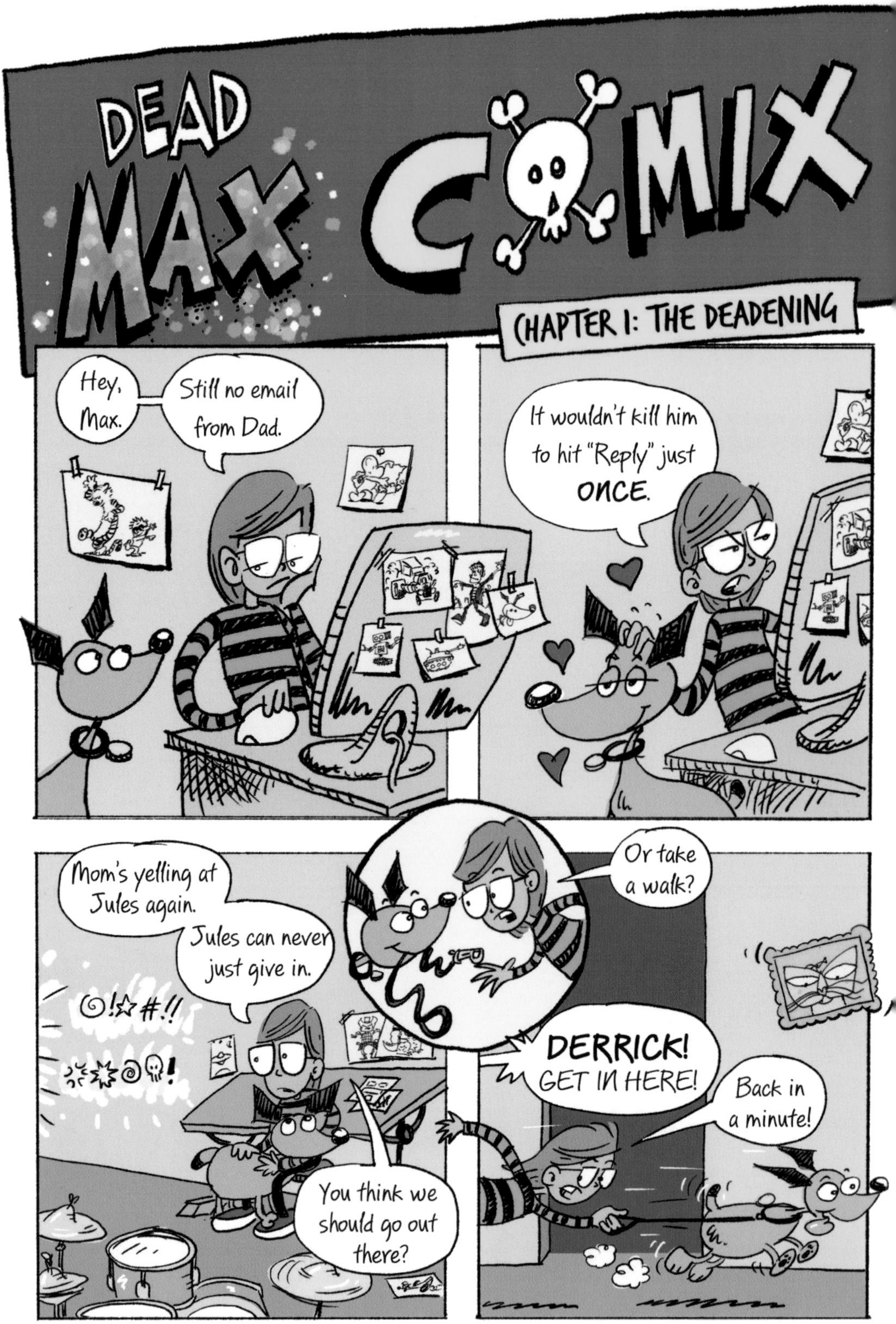
DEAD MAX COMIX
CHAPTER 1: THE DEADENING
Hey, Max.
Still no email from Dad.
It wouldn't kill him to hit "Reply" just ONCE.
Mom's yelling at Jules again.
Jules can never just give in.
You think we should go out there?
Or take a walk?
DERRICK! GET IN HERE!
Back in a minute!

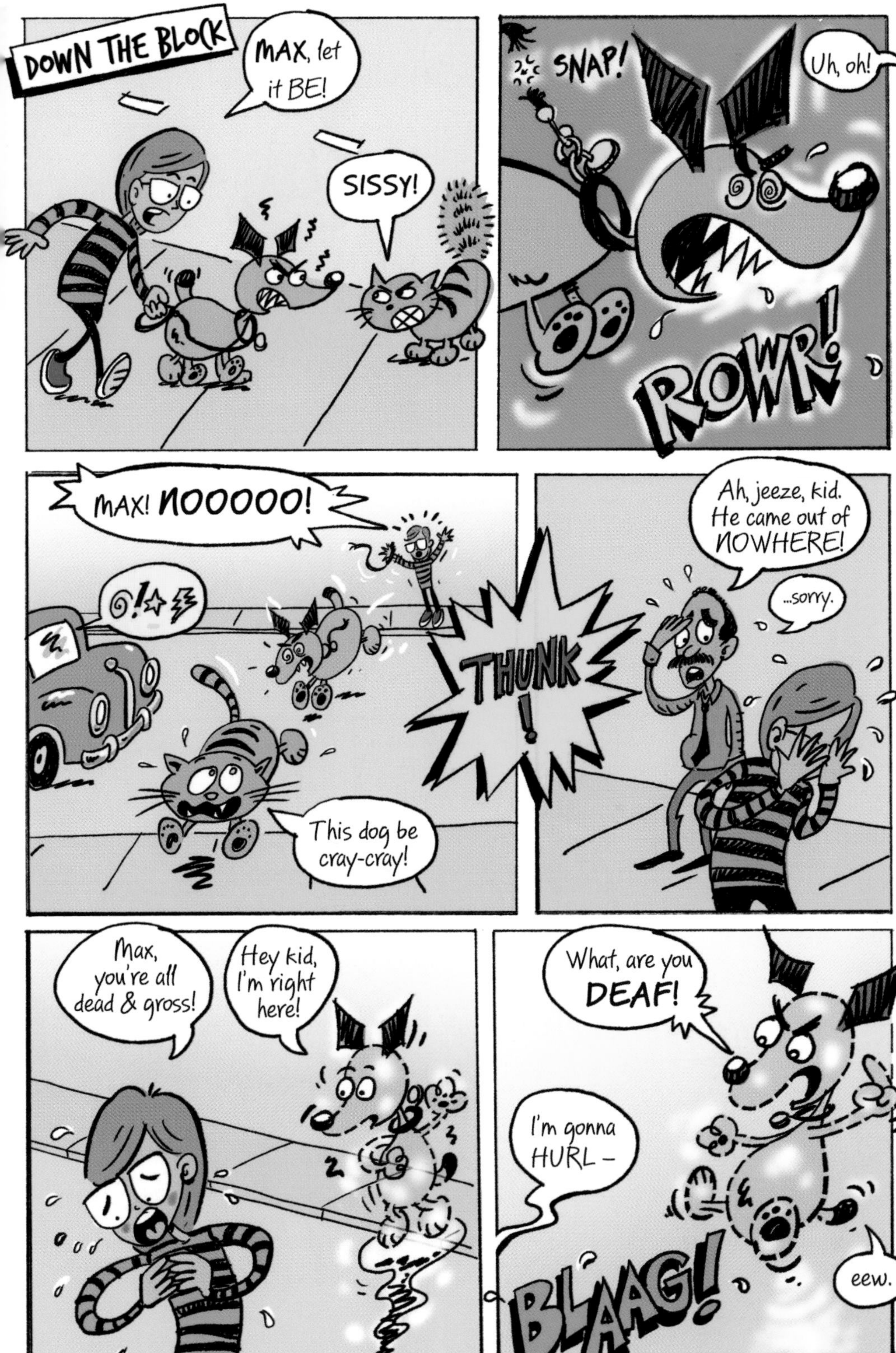
DOWN THE BLOCK
MAX, let it BE!
SISSY!
SNAP!
Uh, oh!
ROWR!
MAX! NOOOOO!
This dog be cray-cray!
THUNK!
Ah, jeeze, kid. He came out of NOWHERE!
...sorry.
Max, you're all dead & gross!
Hey kid, I'm right here!
What, are you DEAF!
I'm gonna HURL –
BLAAG!
eew.

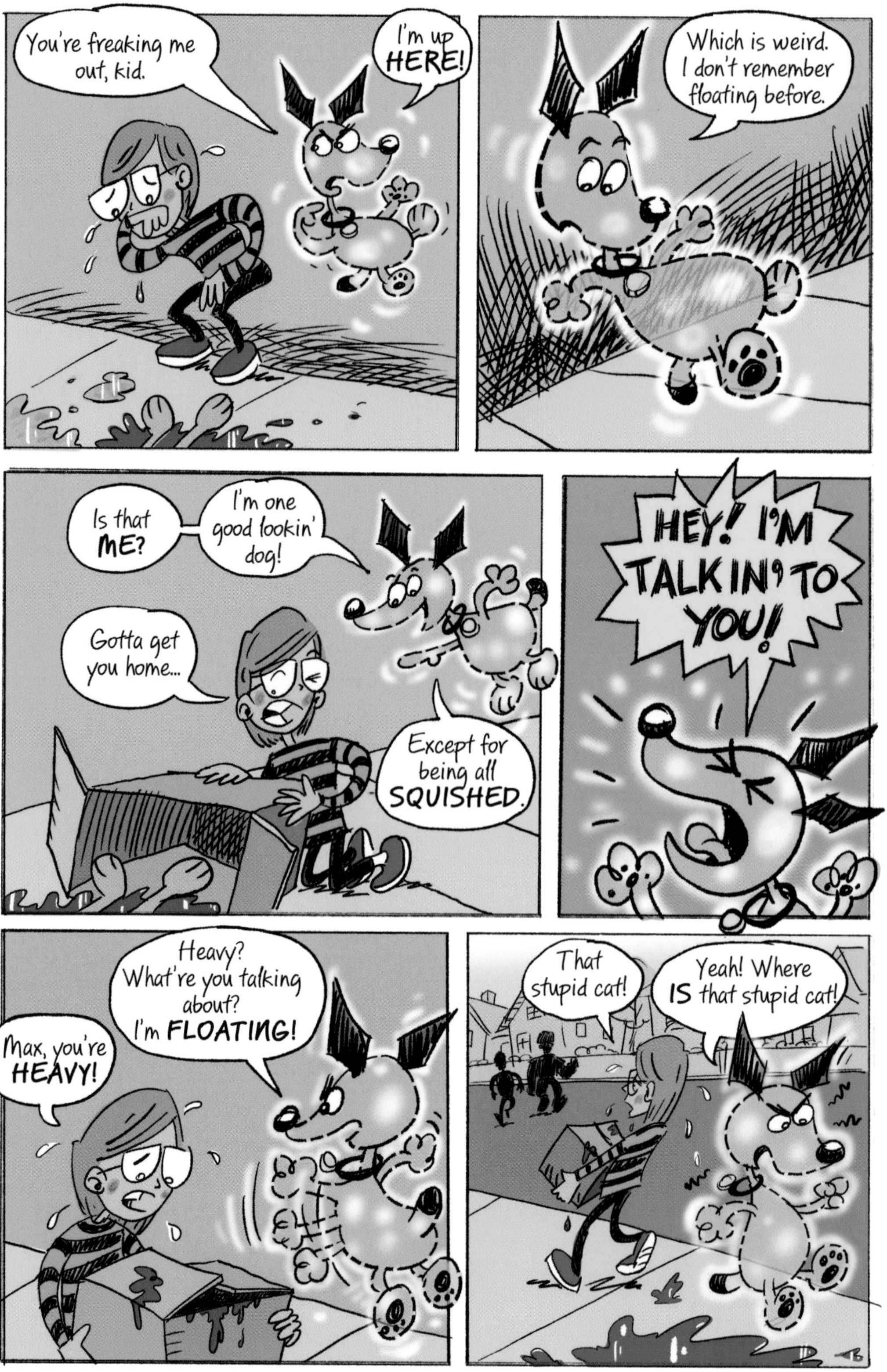
You're freaking me out, kid.
I'm up HERE!
Which is weird. I don't remember floating before.
Is that ME?
I'm one good lookin' dog!
Gotta get you home...
Except for being all SQUISHED.
HEY! I'M TALKIN' TO YOU!
Max, you're HEAVY!
Heavy? What're you talking about? I'm FLOATING!
That stupid cat!
Yeah! Where IS that stupid cat!

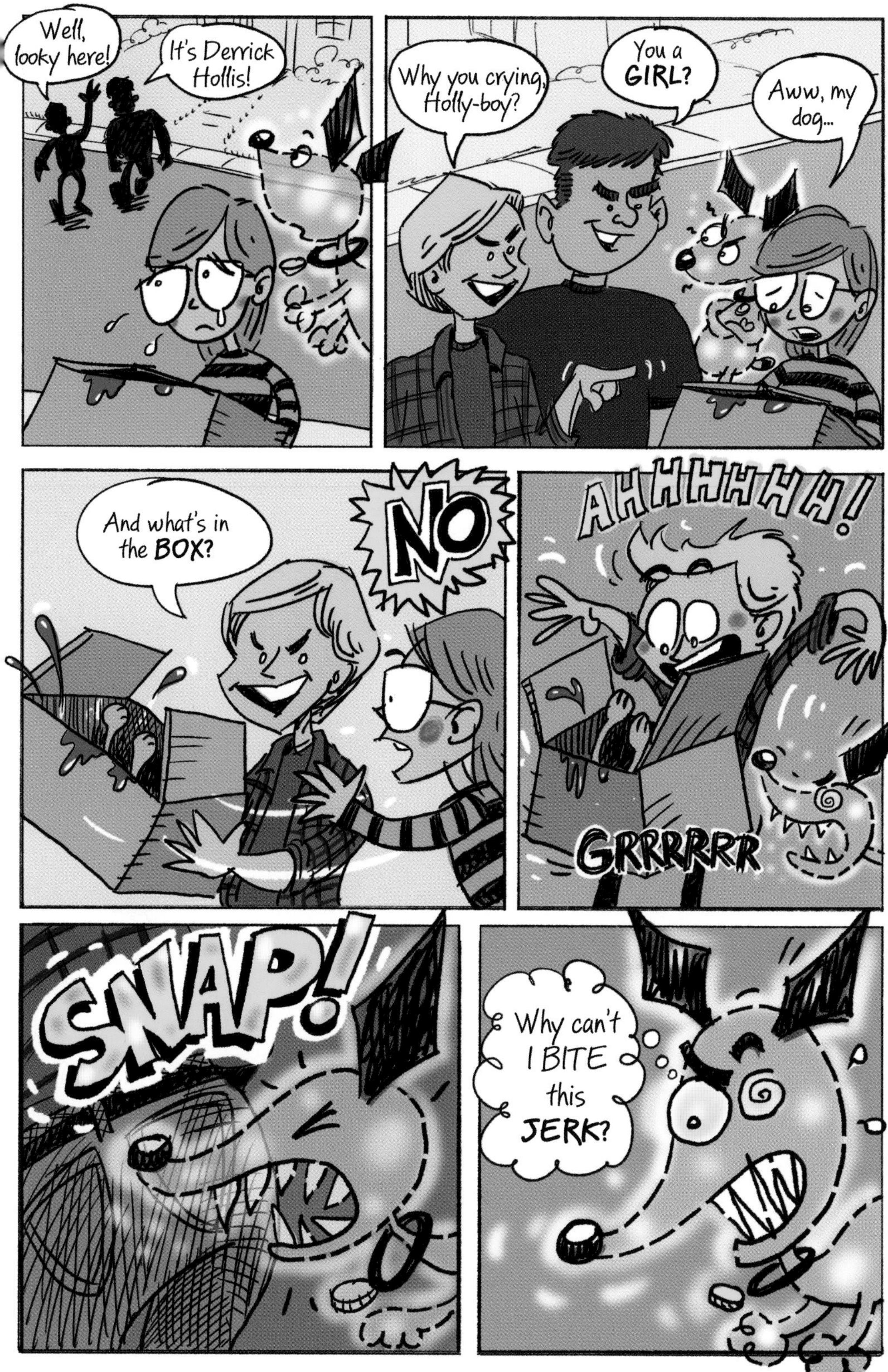
Well, looky here!
It's Derrick Hollis!
Why you crying, Holly-boy?
You a GIRL?
Aww, my dog...
And what's in the BOX?
NO
AHHHHHH!
GRRRRRR
SNAP!
Why can't I BITE this JERK?

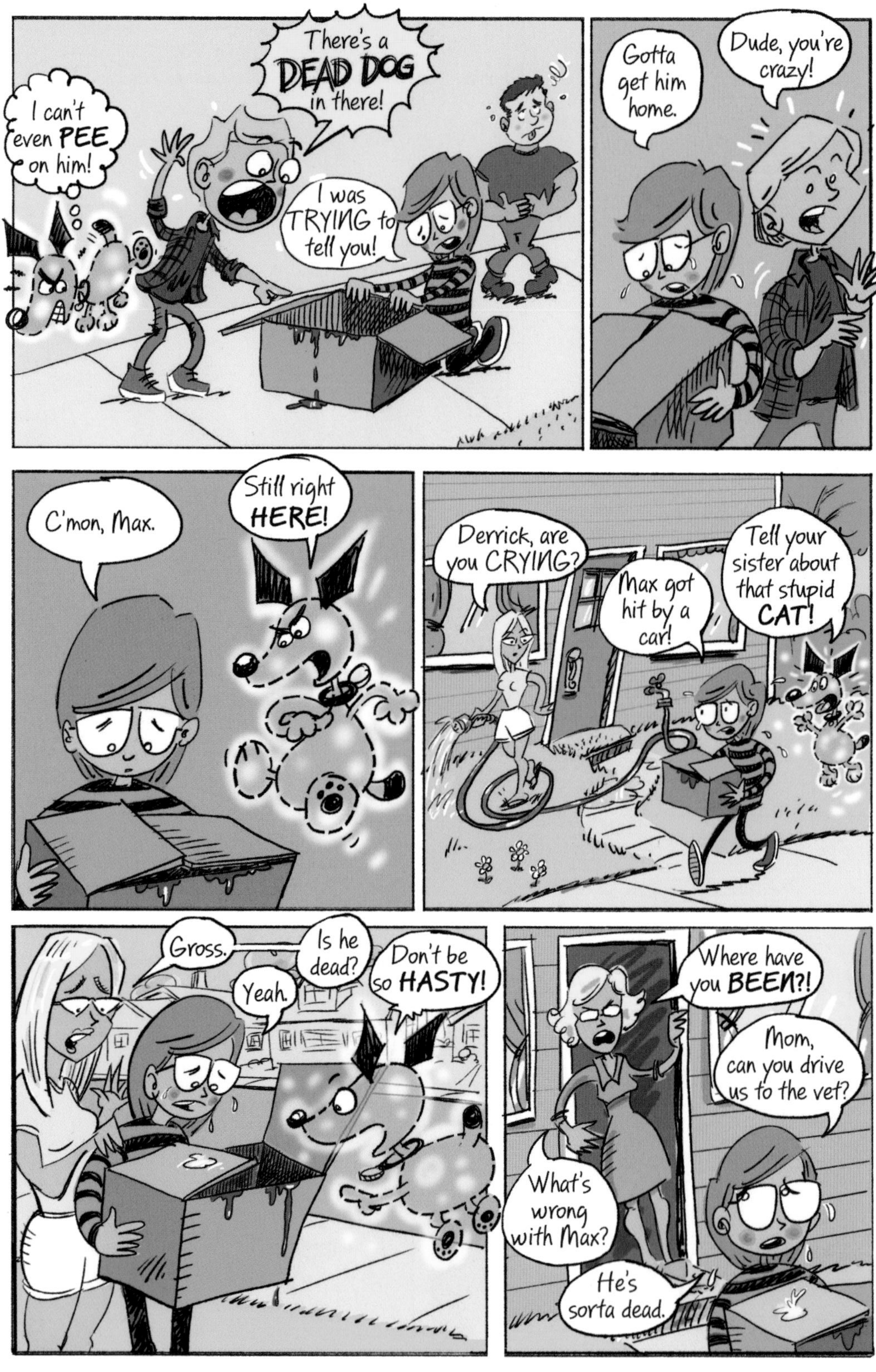

There's a DEAD DOG in there!
I can't even PEE on him!
I was TRYING to tell you!
Gotta get him home.
Dude, you're crazy!
C'mon, Max.
Still right HERE!
Derrick, are you CRYING?
Max got hit by a car!
Tell your sister about that stupid CAT!
Gross.
Is he dead?
Yeah.
Don't be so HASTY!
Where have you BEEN?!
Mom, can you drive us to the vet?
What's wrong with Max?
He's sorta dead.

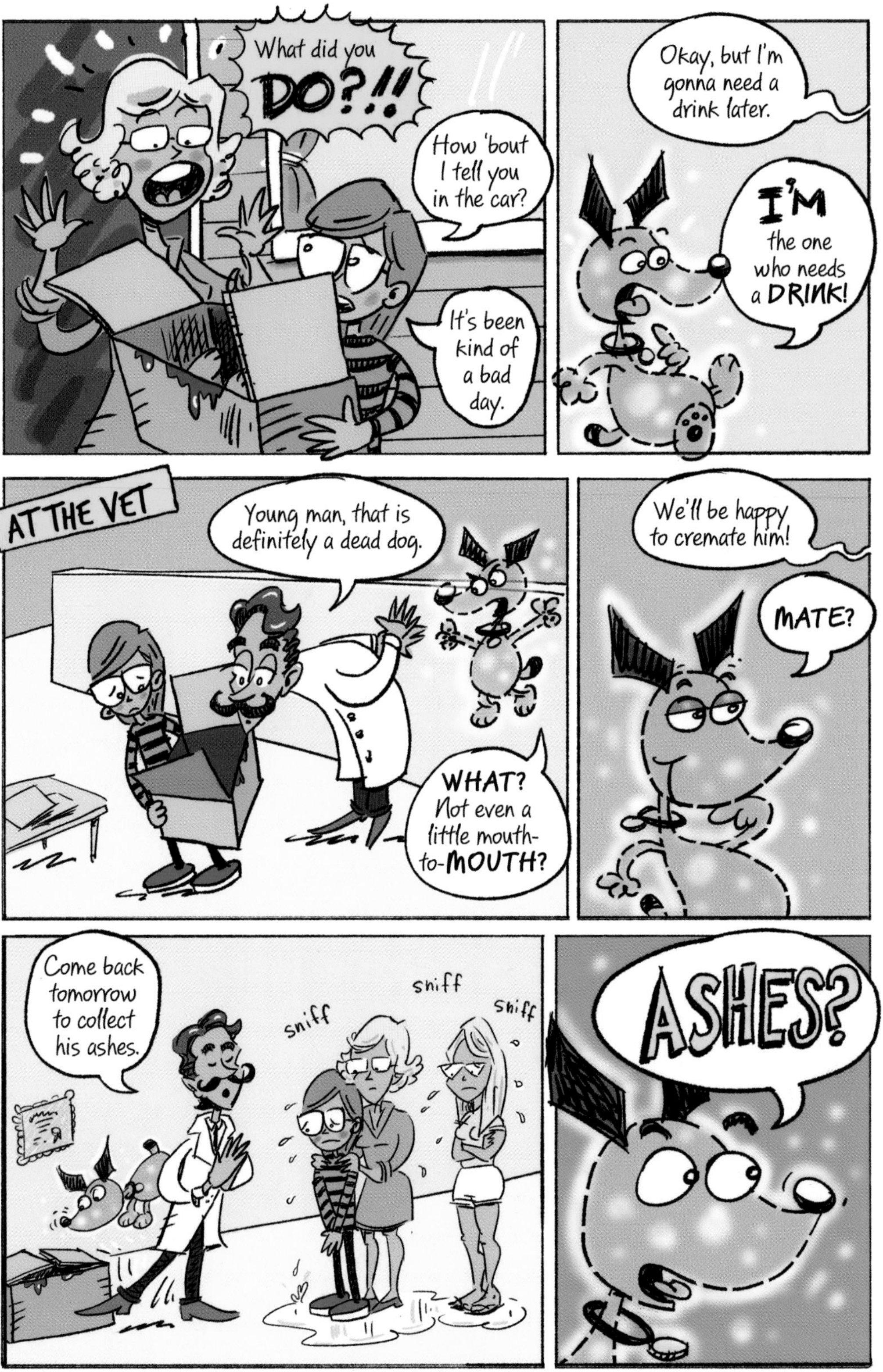
What did you DO?!!
How 'bout I tell you in the car?
It's been kind of a bad day.
Okay, but I'm gonna need a drink later.
I'M the one who needs a DRINK!
AT THE VET
Young man, that is definitely a dead dog.
WHAT? Not even a little mouth-to-MOUTH?
We'll be happy to cremate him!
MATE?
Come back tomorrow to collect his ashes.
sniff
sniff
sniff
ASHES?

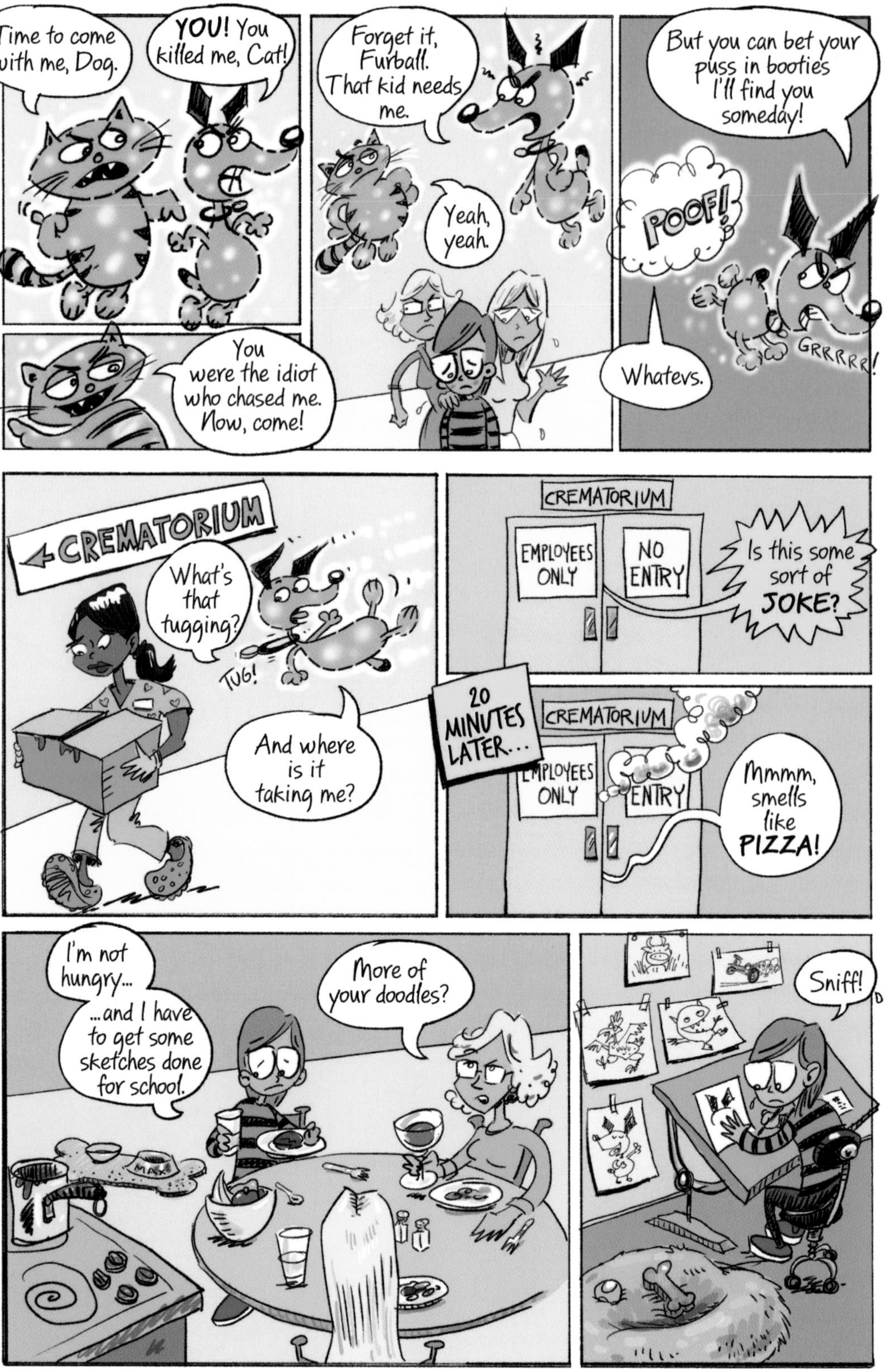
Time to come with me, Dog.
YOU! You killed me, Cat!
You were the idiot who chased me. Now, come!
Forget it, Furball. That kid needs me.
Yeah, yeah.
But you can bet your puss in booties I'll find you someday!
POOF!
Whatevs.
GRRRRRR!
CREMATORIUM
What's that tugging?
TUG!
And where is it taking me?
CREMATORIUM
EMPLOYEES ONLY
NO ENTRY
Is this some sort of JOKE?
20 MINUTES LATER...
CREMATORIUM
EMPLOYEES ONLY
ENTRY
Mmmm, smells like PIZZA!
I'm not hungry...
...and I have to get some sketches done for school.
More of your doodles?
MAX
Sniff!

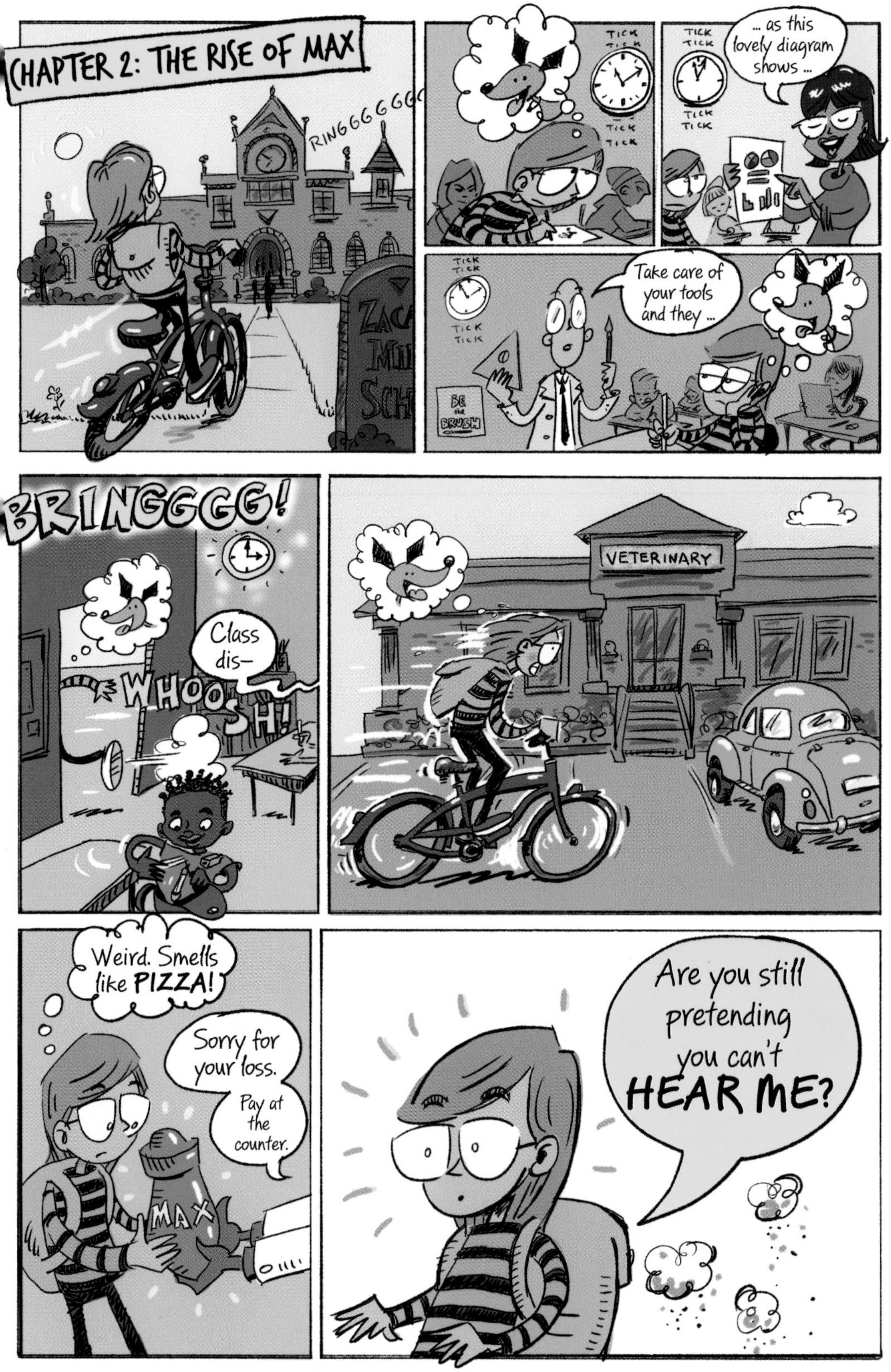
CHAPTER 2: THE RISE OF MAX
RINGGGGGGG
ZACA
MID
SCH
TICK TICK
TICK TICK
TICK TICK
TICK TICK
... as this lovely diagram shows ...
TICK TICK
TICK TICK
Take care of your tools and they ...
BE the BRUSH
BRINGGGG!
Class dis—
WHOOSH!
VETERINARY
Weird. Smells like PIZZA!
Sorry for your loss.
Pay at the counter.
MAX
Are you still pretending you can't HEAR ME?

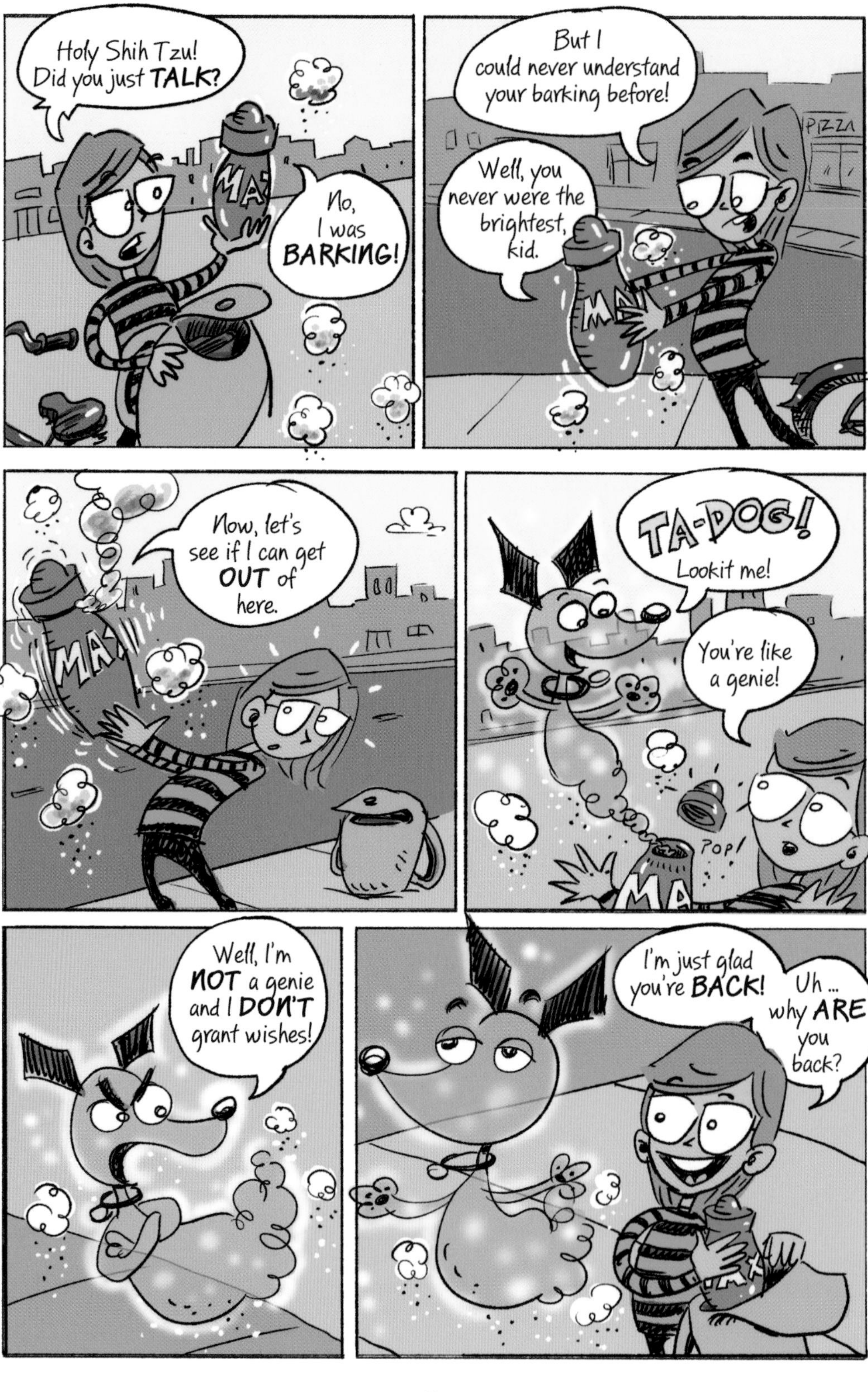
Holy Shih Tzu! Did you just TALK?
No, I was BARKING!
But I could never understand your barking before!
Well, you never were the brightest, kid.
PIZZA
Now, let's see if I can get OUT of here.
TA-DOG! Lookit me!
You're like a genie!
POP!
Well, I'm NOT a genie and I DON'T grant wishes!
I'm just glad you're BACK!
Uh ... why ARE you back?

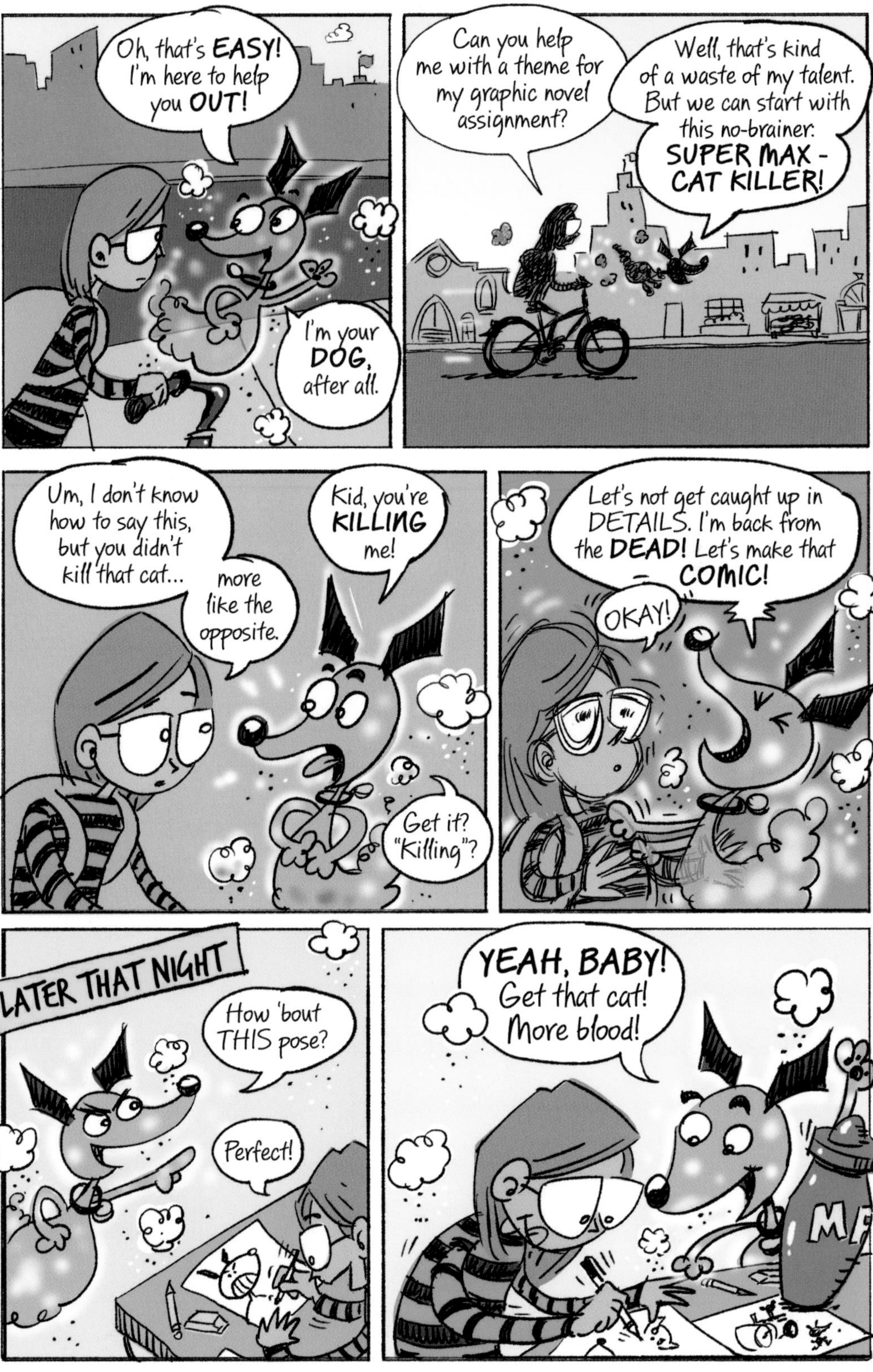

Oh, that's EASY! I'm here to help you OUT!
I'm your DOG, after all.
Can you help me with a theme for my graphic novel assignment?
Well, that's kind of a waste of my talent. But we can start with this no-brainer: SUPER MAX - CAT KILLER!
Um, I don't know how to say this, but you didn't kill that cat...
more like the opposite.
Kid, you're KILLING me!
Get it? "Killing"?
Let's not get caught up in DETAILS. I'm back from the DEAD! Let's make that COMIC!
OKAY!
LATER THAT NIGHT
How 'bout THIS pose?
Perfect!
YEAH, BABY! Get that cat! More blood!
MF

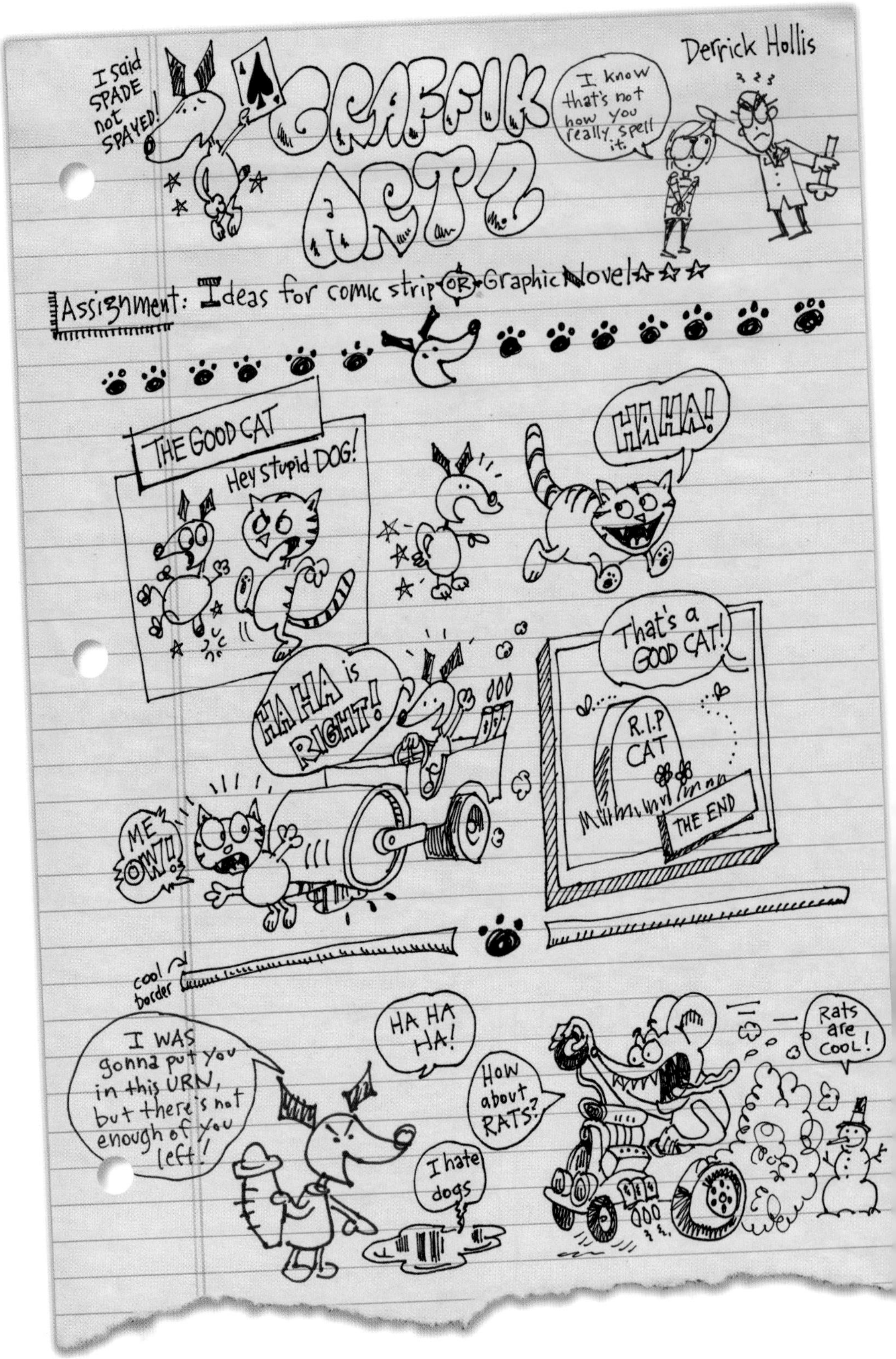

Derrick Hollis
I said SPADE not SPAYED!
GRAFFIK ARTZ
I know that's not how you really spell it.
Assignment: Ideas for comic strip OR Graphic Novel
THE GOOD CAT
Hey stupid DOG!
HAHA!
HAHA is RIGHT!
MEOW!!
That's a GOOD CAT!
R.I.P CAT
THE END
cool border
I WAS gonna put you in this URN, but there's not enough of you left!
HA HA HA!
How about RATS?
I hate dogs
Rats are COOL!

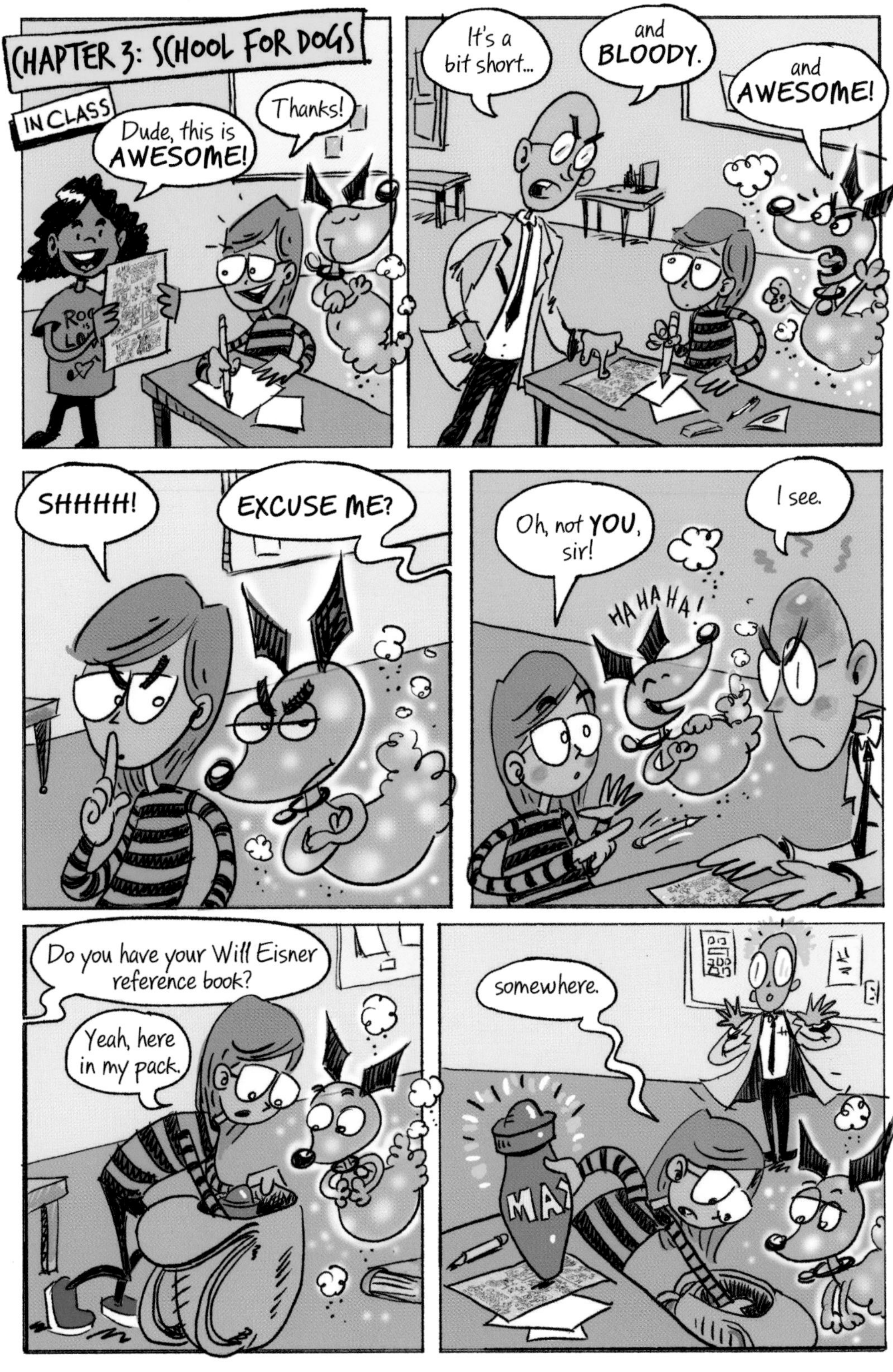
CHAPTER 3: SCHOOL FOR DOGS
IN CLASS
Dude, this is AWESOME!
Thanks!
It's a bit short...
and BLOODY.
and AWESOME!
SHHHH!
EXCUSE ME?
Oh, not YOU, sir!
I see.
HAHAHA!
Do you have your Will Eisner reference book?
Yeah, here in my pack.
somewhere.
MA

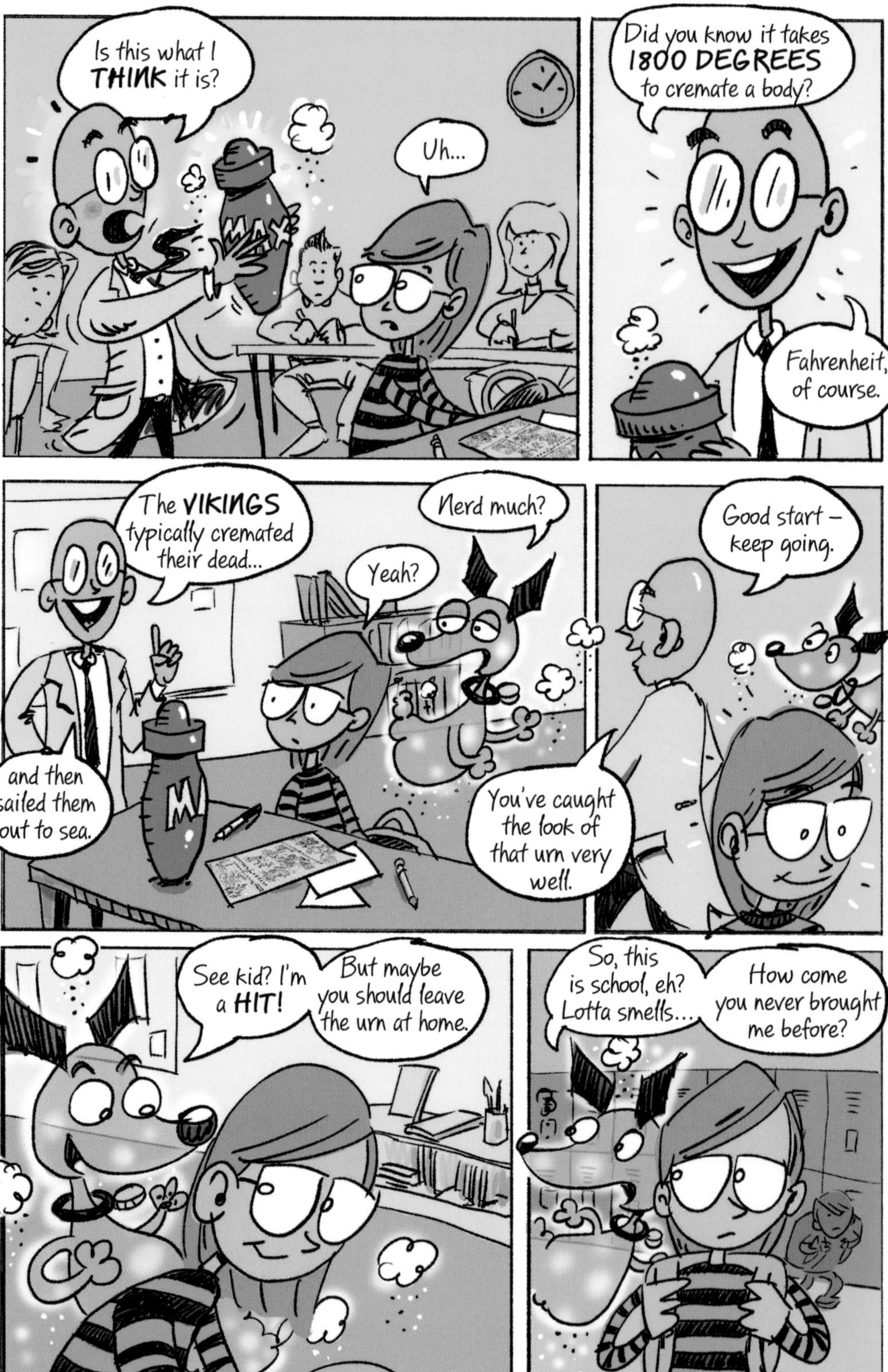
Is this what I THINK it is?
Uh...
Did you know it takes 1800 DEGREES to cremate a body?
Fahrenheit, of course.
The VIKINGS typically cremated their dead...
and then sailed them out to sea.
Yeah?
Nerd much?
Good start – keep going.
You've caught the look of that urn very well.
See kid? I'm a HIT!
But maybe you should leave the urn at home.
So, this is school, eh? Lotta smells...
How come you never brought me before?

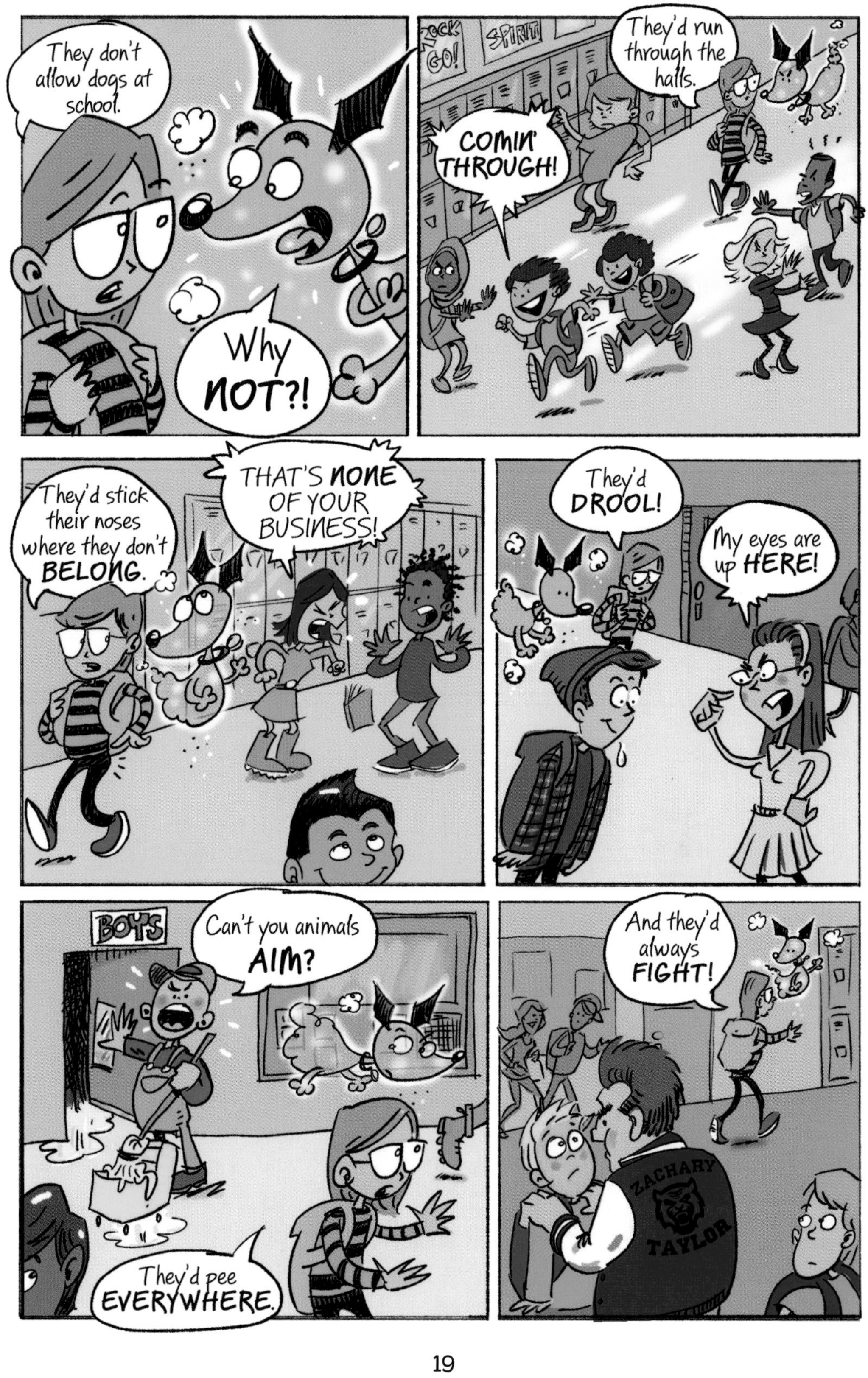
They don't allow dogs at school.
Why NOT?!
SPIRIT
They'd run through the halls.
COMIN' THROUGH!
They'd stick their noses where they don't BELONG.
THAT'S NONE OF YOUR BUSINESS!
They'd DROOL!
My eyes are up HERE!
BOYS
Can't you animals AIM?
They'd pee EVERYWHERE.
And they'd always FIGHT!
ZACHARY
TAYLOR

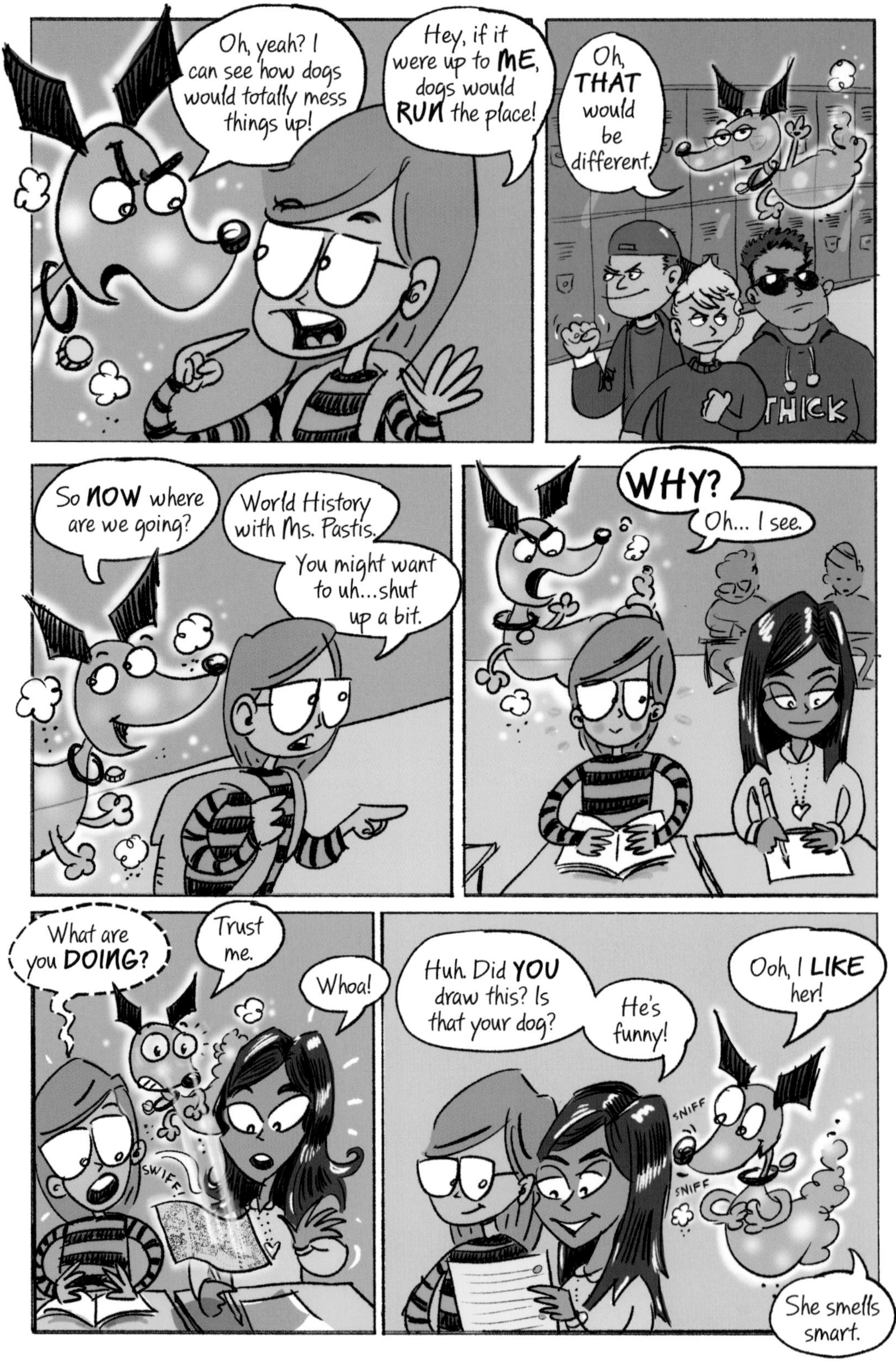

Oh, yeah? I can see how dogs would totally mess things up!
Hey, if it were up to ME, dogs would RUN the place!
Oh, THAT would be different.
THICK
So NOW where are we going?
World History with Ms. Pastis.
You might want to uh...shut up a bit.
WHY?
Oh... I see.
What are you DOING?
Trust me.
Whoa!
SNIFF!
Huh. Did YOU draw this? Is that your dog?
He's funny!
Ooh, I LIKE her!
SNIFF
SNIFF
She smells smart.

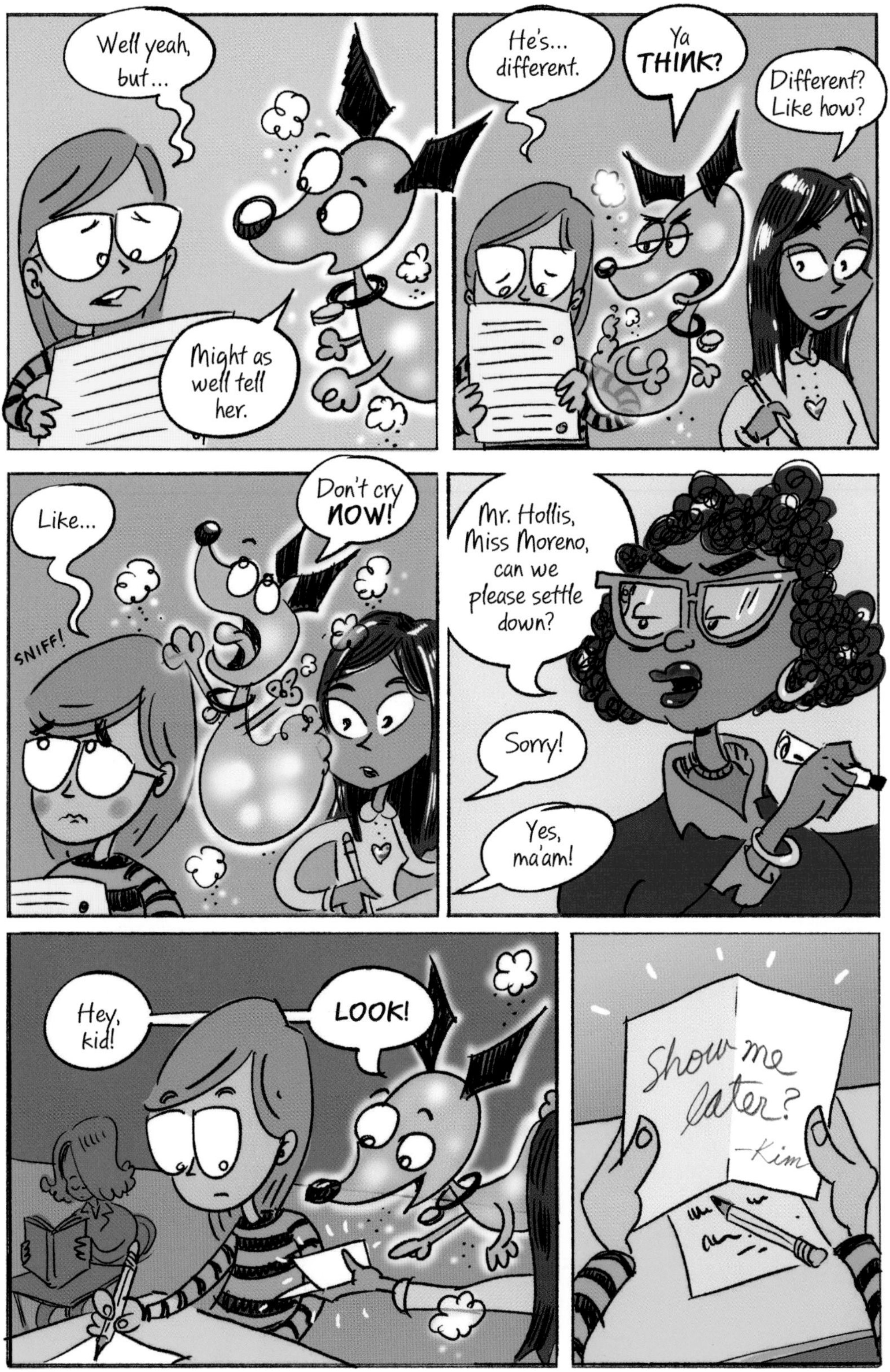
Well yeah, but...
Might as well tell her.
He's... different.
Ya THINK?
Different? Like how?
Like...
Don't cry NOW!
SNIFF!
Mr. Hollis, Miss Moreno, can we please settle down?
Sorry!
Yes, ma'am!
Hey, kid!
LOOK!
Show me later?
-Kim

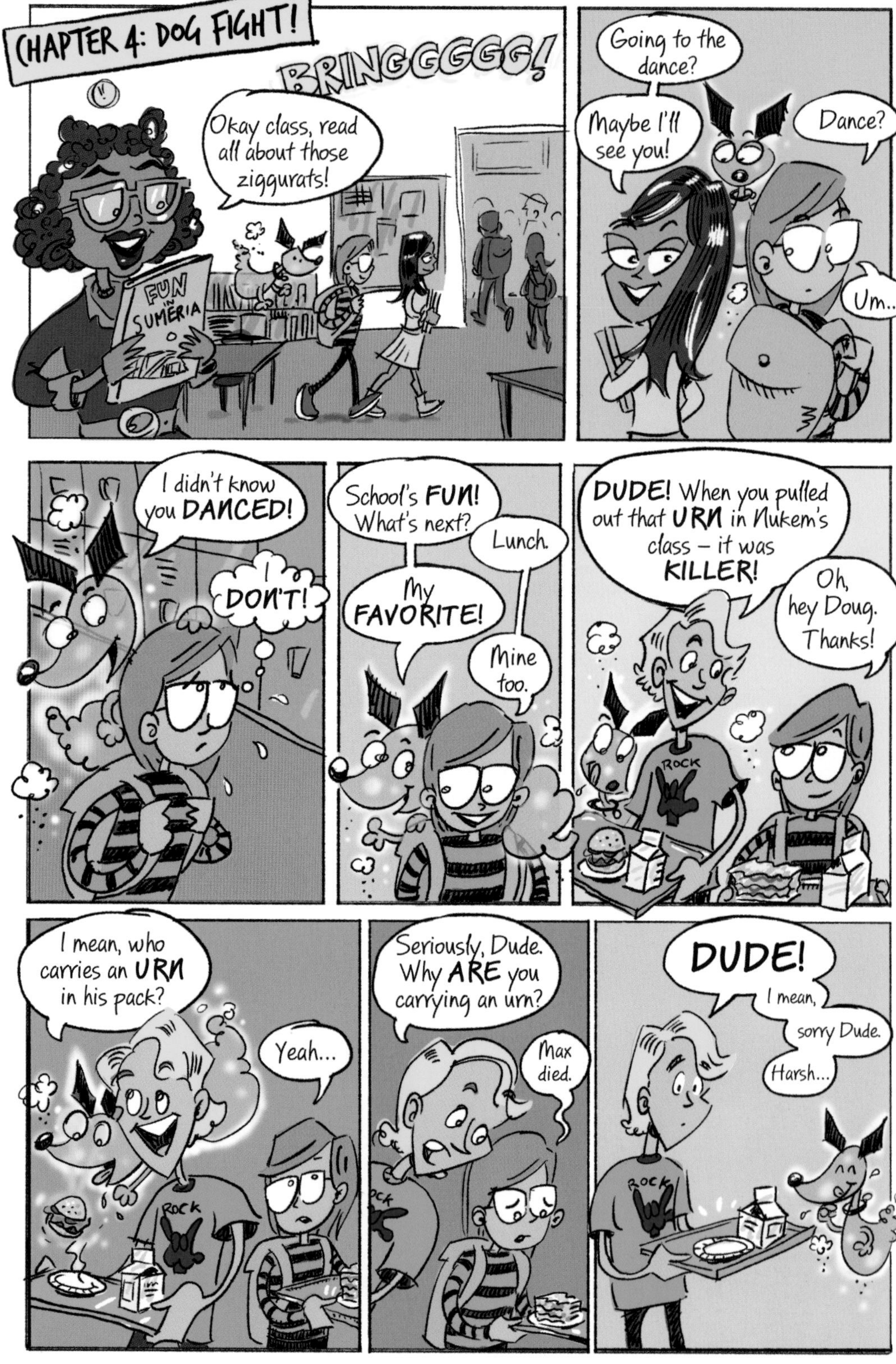
CHAPTER 4: DOG FIGHT!
BRINGGGGG!
Okay class, read all about those ziggurats!
FUN IN SUMERIA
Going to the dance?
Maybe I'll see you!
Dance?
Um...
I didn't know you DANCED!
I DON'T!
School's FUN! What's next?
Lunch.
My FAVORITE!
Mine too.
DUDE! When you pulled out that URN in Nukem's class – it was KILLER!
Oh, hey Doug. Thanks!
ROCK
I mean, who carries an URN in his pack?
Yeah...
Seriously, Dude. Why ARE you carrying an urn?
Max died.
DUDE!
I mean, sorry Dude.
Harsh...

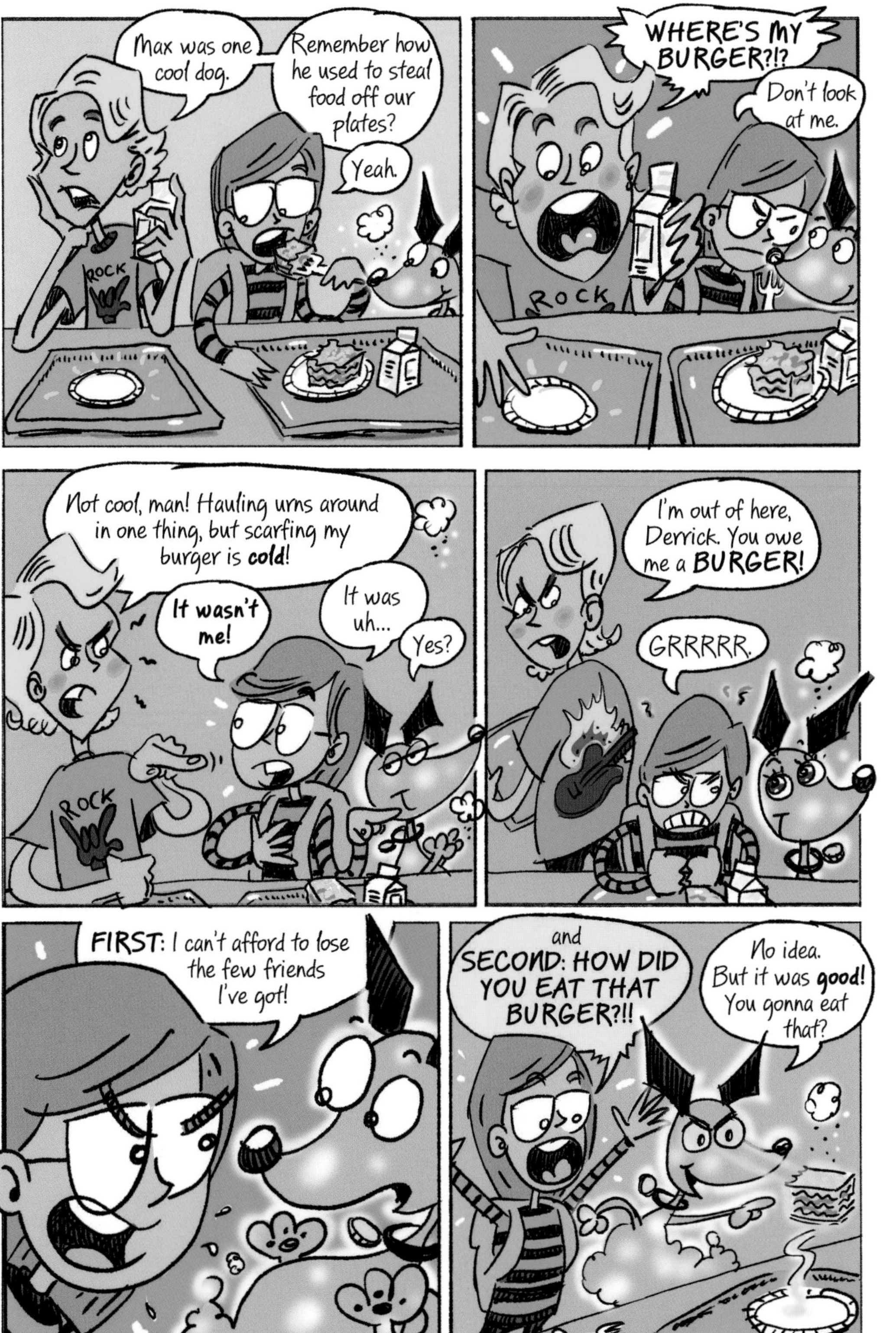
Max was one cool dog.
Remember how he used to steal food off our plates?
Yeah.
WHERE'S MY BURGER?!?
Don't look at me.
Not cool, man! Hauling urns around in one thing, but scarfing my burger is **cold**!
It wasn't me!
It was uh...
Yes?
I'm out of here, Derrick. You owe me a **BURGER**!
GRRRRR.
FIRST: I can't afford to lose the few friends I've got!
and
SECOND: HOW DID YOU EAT THAT BURGER?!!
No idea. But it was **good**! You gonna eat that?

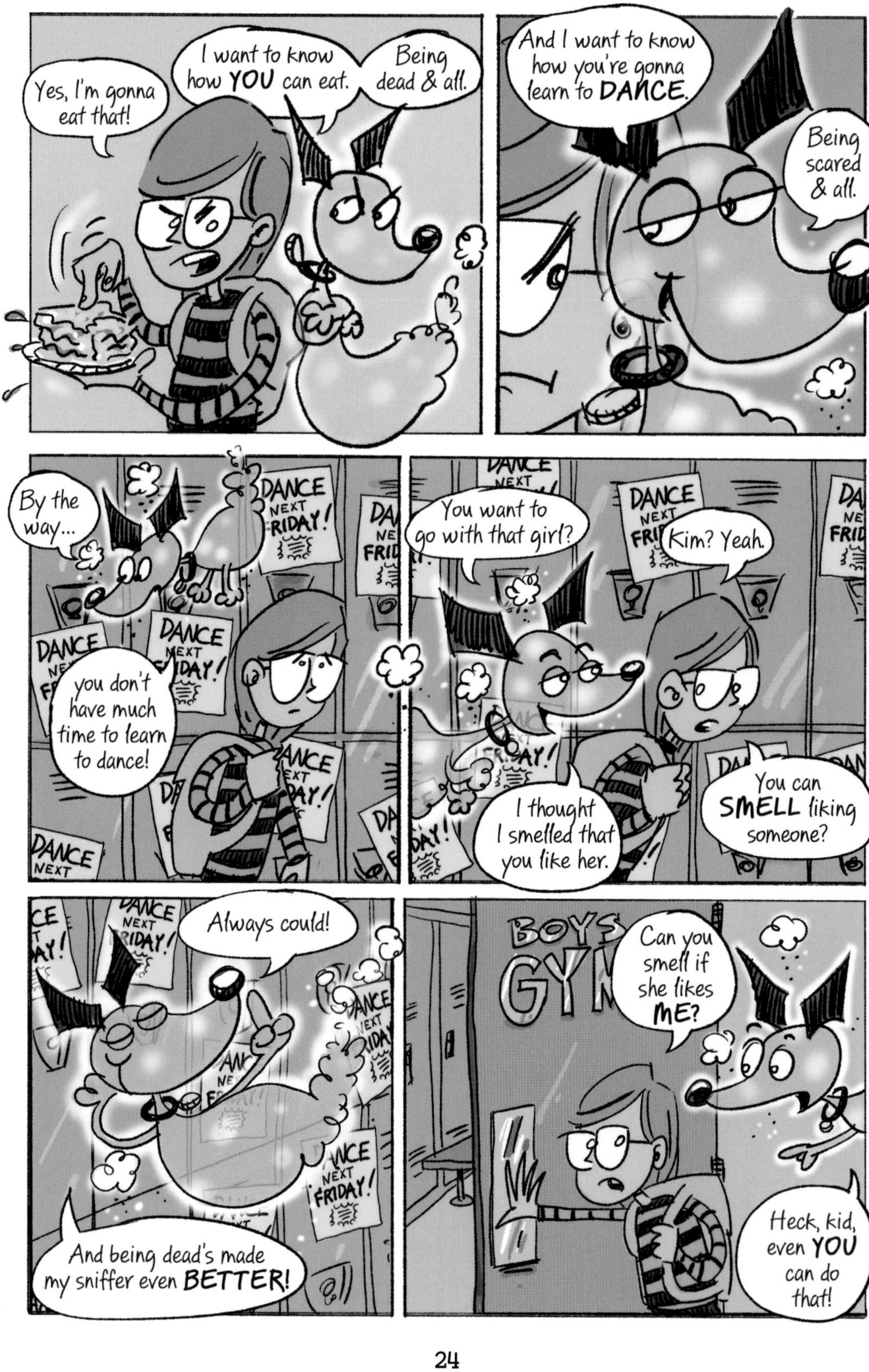
Yes, I'm gonna eat that!
I want to know how YOU can eat.
Being dead & all.
And I want to know how you're gonna learn to DANCE.
Being scared & all.
By the way...
you don't have much time to learn to dance!
You want to go with that girl?
Kim? Yeah.
I thought I smelled that you like her.
You can SMELL liking someone?
Always could!
And being dead's made my sniffer even BETTER!
Can you smell if she likes ME?
Heck, kid, even YOU can do that!
BOYS GYM
DANCE NEXT FRIDAY!

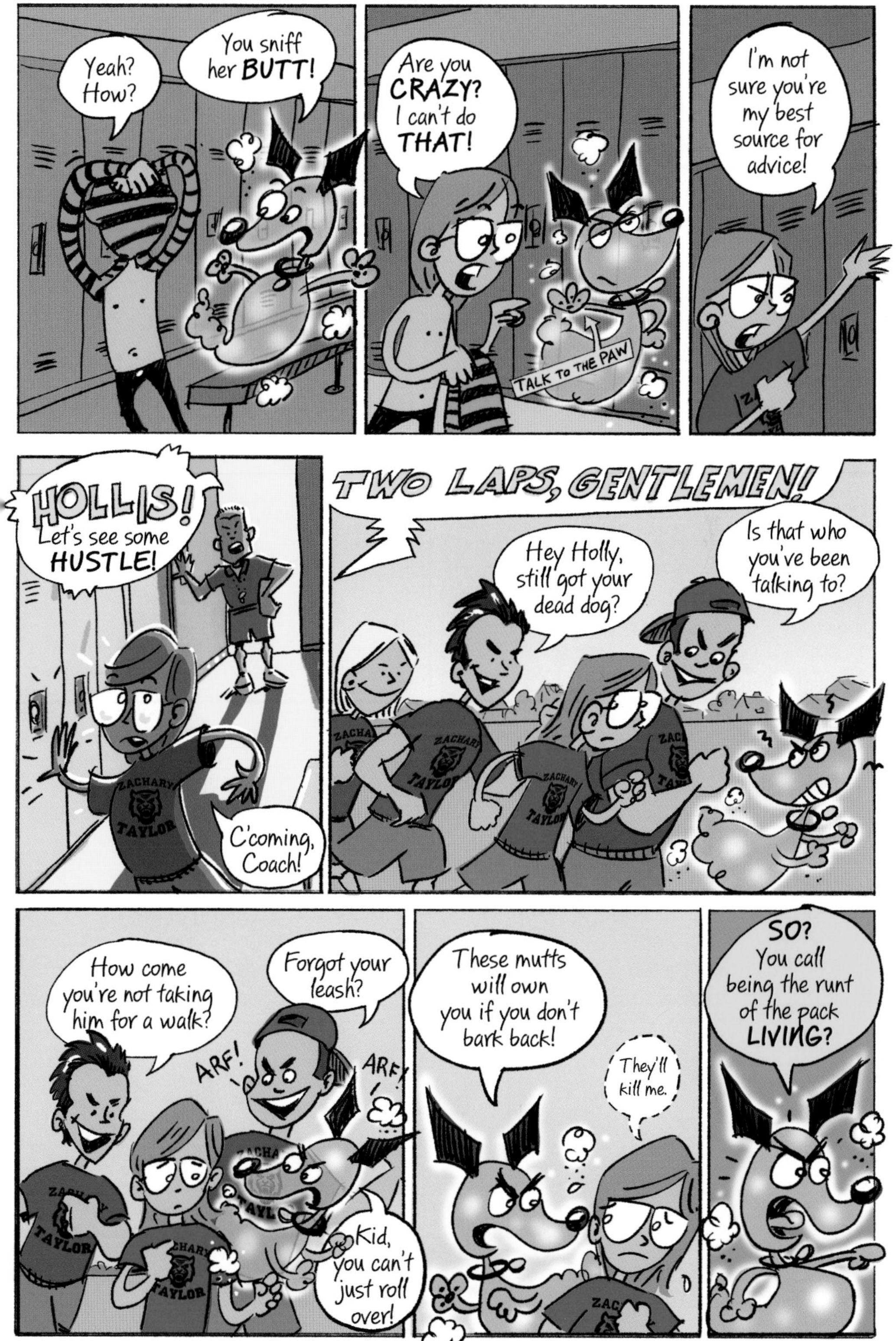
Yeah? How?
You sniff her BUTT!
Are you CRAZY? I can't do THAT!
TALK TO THE PAW
I'm not sure you're my best source for advice!
HOLLIS! Let's see some HUSTLE!
C'coming, Coach!
TWO LAPS, GENTLEMEN!
Hey Holly, still got your dead dog?
Is that who you've been talking to?
ZACHARY TAYLOR
How come you're not taking him for a walk?
Forgot your leash?
ARF!
ARF!
Kid, you can't just roll over!
These mutts will own you if you don't bark back!
They'll kill me.
SO? You call being the runt of the pack LIVING?

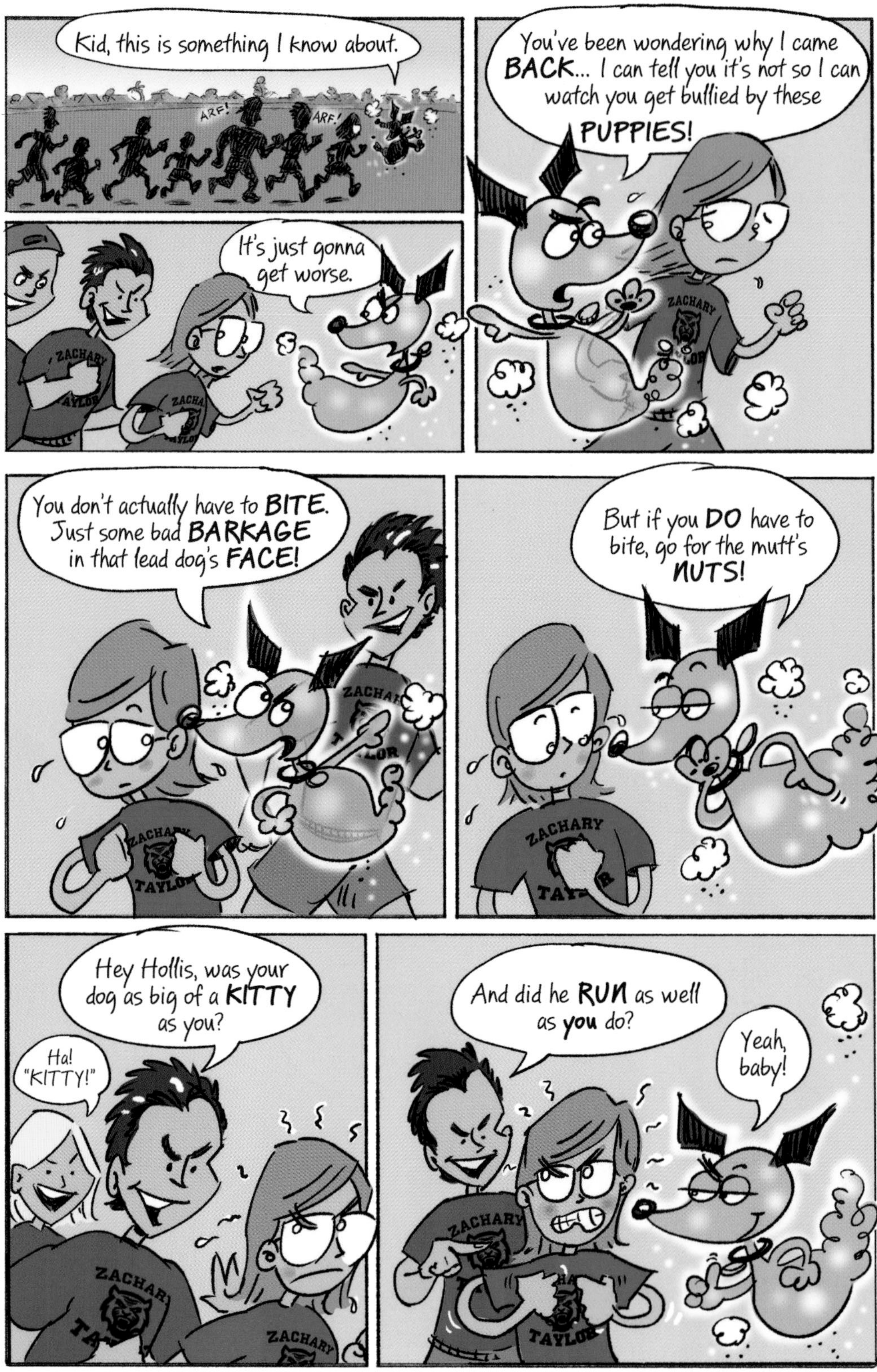
Kid, this is something I know about.
ARF!
ARF!
You've been wondering why I came BACK... I can tell you it's not so I can watch you get bullied by these PUPPIES!
It's just gonna get worse.
You don't actually have to BITE. Just some bad BARKAGE in that lead dog's FACE!
But if you DO have to bite, go for the mutt's NUTS!
Hey Hollis, was your dog as big of a KITTY as you?
Ha! "KITTY!"
And did he RUN as well as you do?
Yeah, baby!

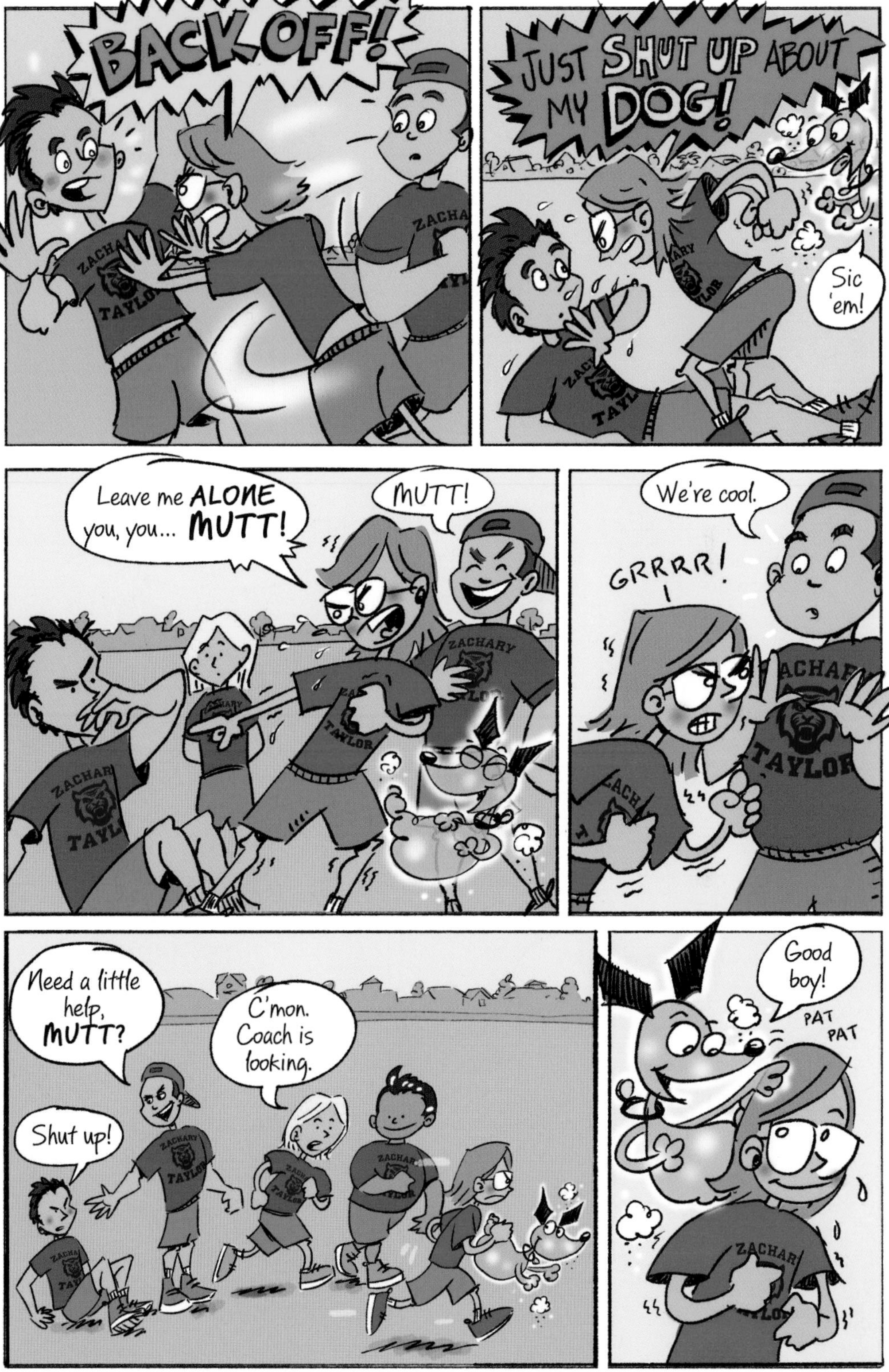
BACK OFF!
JUST SHUT UP ABOUT MY DOG!
Sic 'em!
Leave me ALONE you, you... MUTT!
MUTT!
We're cool.
GRRRR!
Need a little help, MUTT?
C'mon. Coach is looking.
Shut up!
Good boy!
PAT PAT

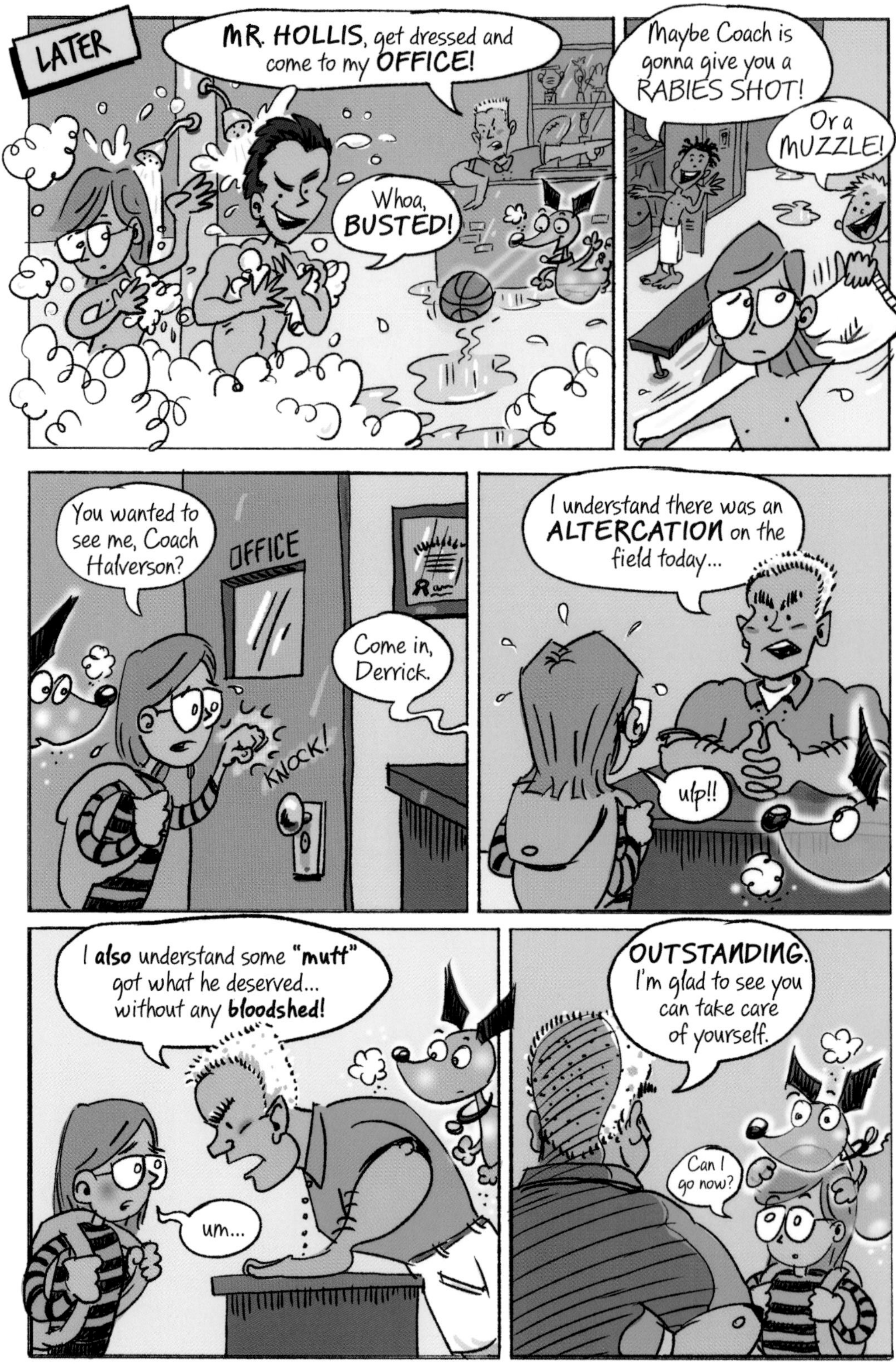
LATER
MR. HOLLIS, get dressed and come to my OFFICE!
Whoa, BUSTED!
Maybe Coach is gonna give you a RABIES SHOT!
Or a MUZZLE!
You wanted to see me, Coach Halverson?
OFFICE
KNOCK!
Come in, Derrick.
I understand there was an ALTERCATION on the field today...
ulp!!
I also understand some "mutt" got what he deserved... without any bloodshed!
um...
OUTSTANDING. I'm glad to see you can take care of yourself.
Can I go now?

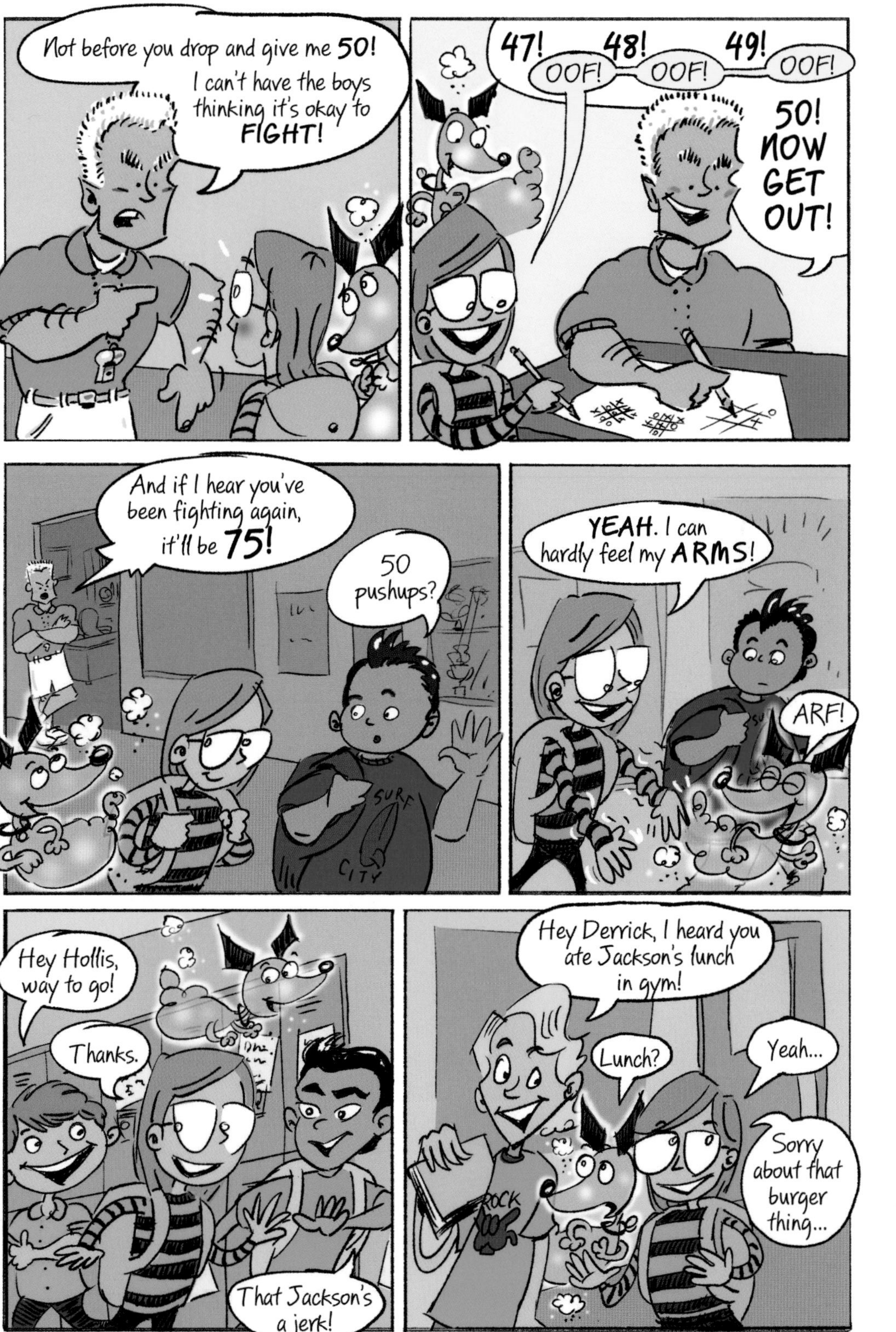
Not before you drop and give me 50!
I can't have the boys thinking it's okay to FIGHT!
47!
OOF!
48!
OOF!
49!
OOF!
50! NOW GET OUT!
And if I hear you've been fighting again, it'll be 75!
50 pushups?
YEAH. I can hardly feel my ARMS!
ARF!
Hey Hollis, way to go!
Thanks.
That Jackson's a jerk!
Hey Derrick, I heard you ate Jackson's lunch in gym!
Lunch?
Yeah...
Sorry about that burger thing...

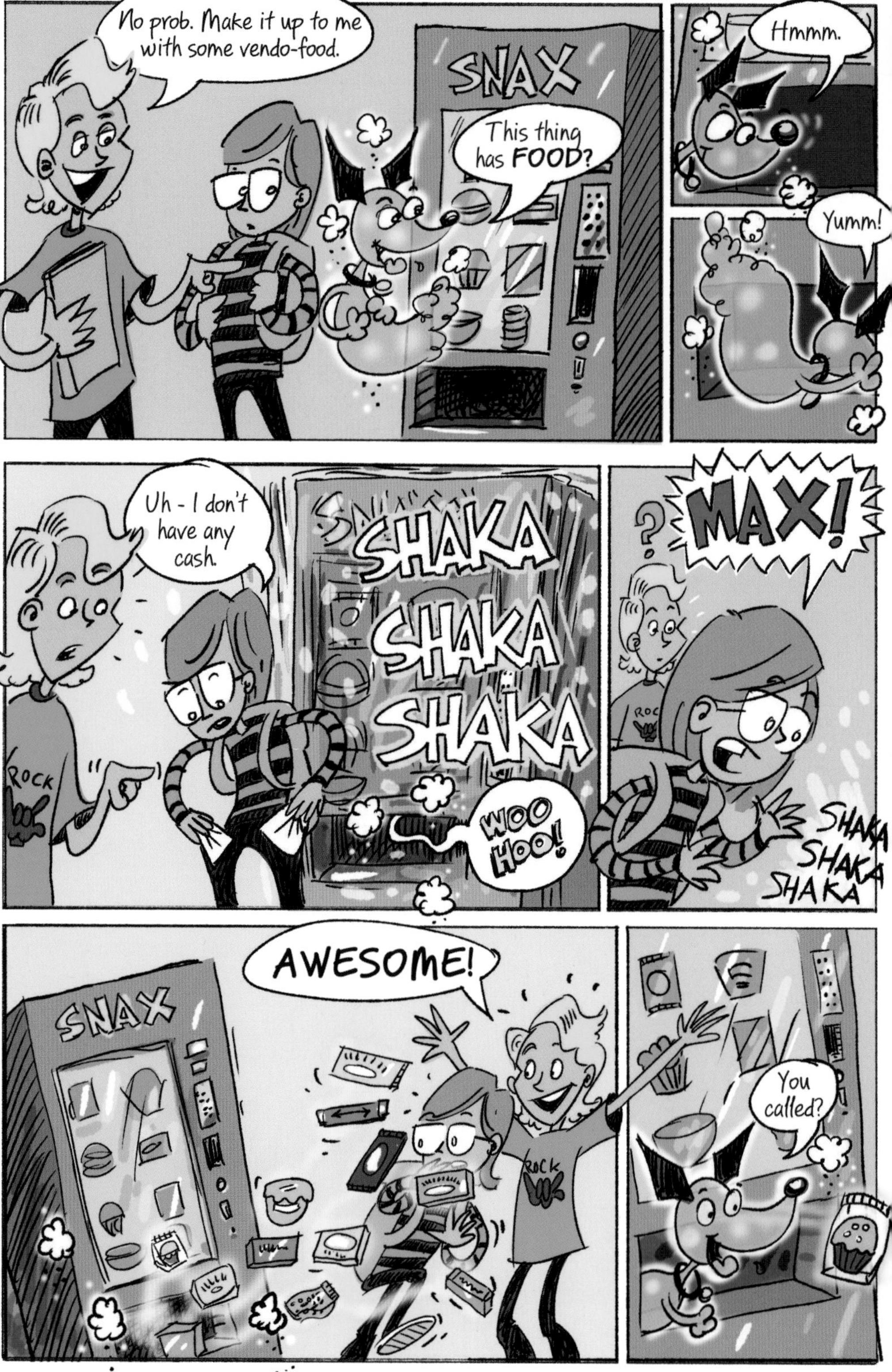
No prob. Make it up to me with some vendo-food.
SNAX
This thing has FOOD?
Hmmm.
Yumm!
Uh - I don't have any cash.
SHAKA SHAKA SHAKA
WOO HOO!
MAX!
SHAKA SHAKA SHAKA
AWESOME!
SNAX
You called?

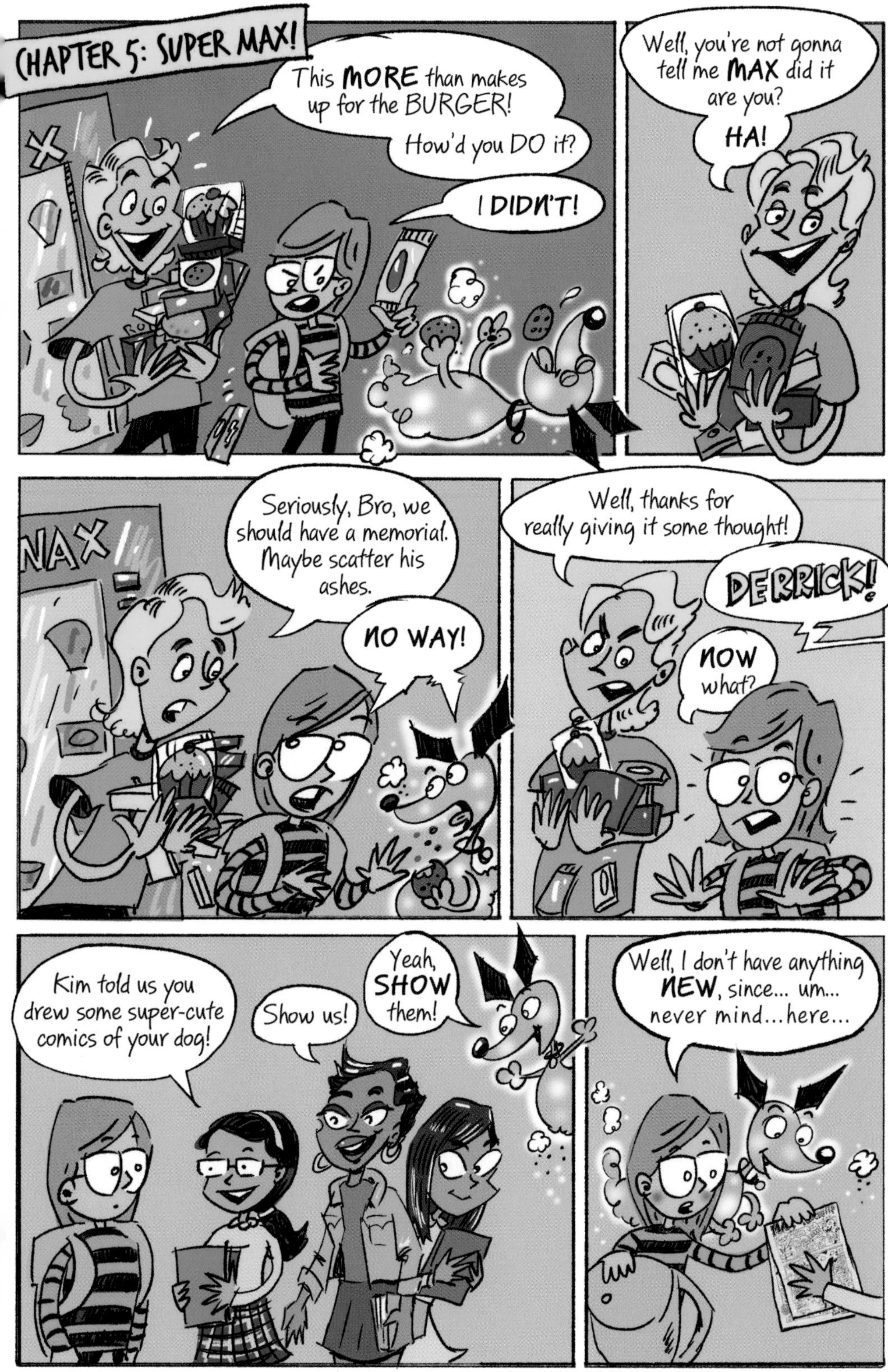
CHAPTER 5: SUPER MAX!
This MORE than makes up for the BURGER!
How'd you DO it?
I DIDN'T!
Well, you're not gonna tell me MAX did it are you?
HA!
Seriously, Bro, we should have a memorial. Maybe scatter his ashes.
NO WAY!
Well, thanks for really giving it some thought!
DERRICK!
NOW what?
Kim told us you drew some super-cute comics of your dog!
Show us!
Yeah, SHOW them!
Well, I don't have anything NEW, since... um... never mind...here...

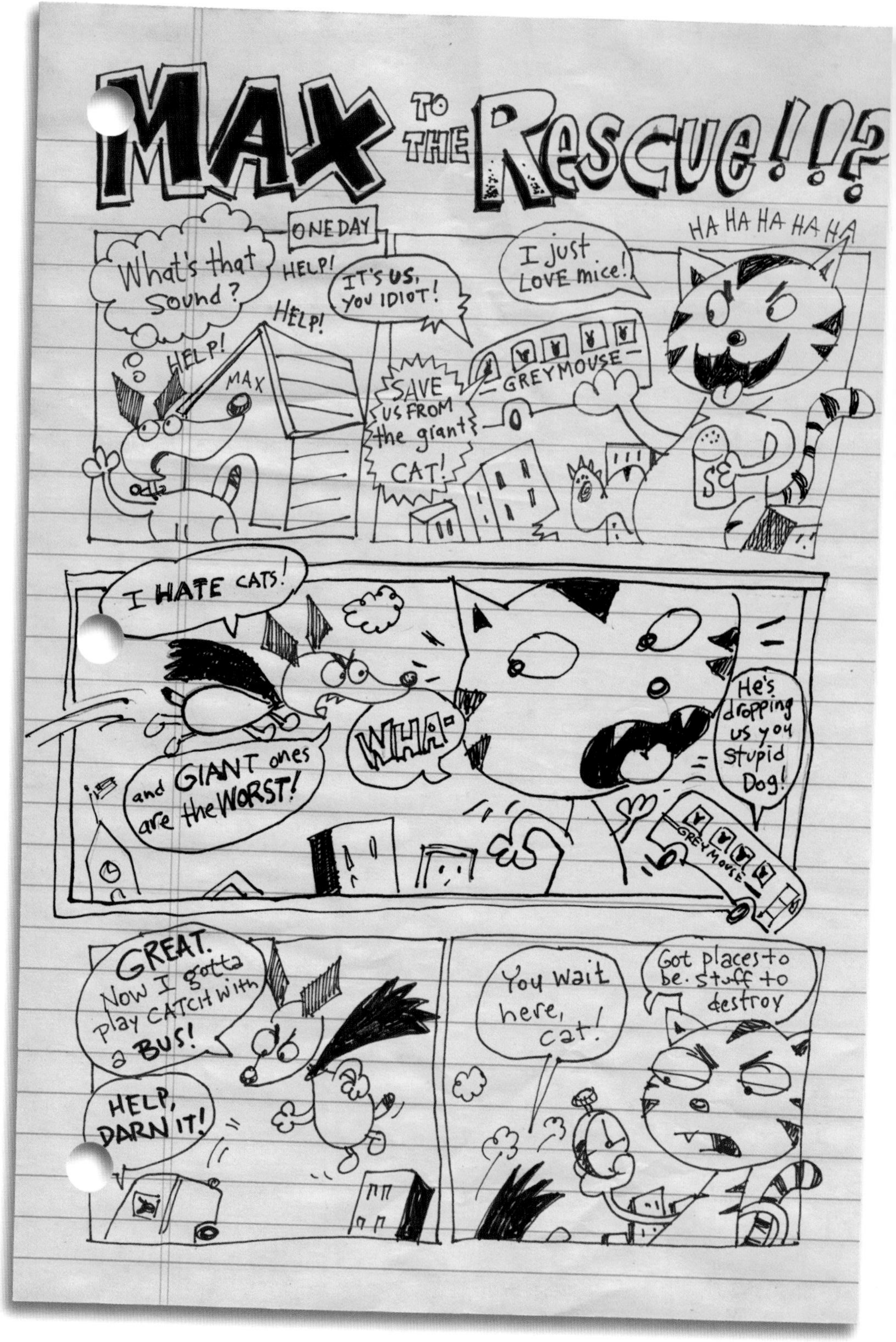
MAX TO THE RESCUE!!?
ONE DAY
What's that sound?
HELP!
HELP!
HELP!
MAX
IT'S US, YOU IDIOT!
SAVE US FROM the giant CAT!
GREYMOUSE
I just LOVE mice!
HA HA HA HA HA
I HATE CATS!
and GIANT ones are the WORST!
WHA?
He's dropping us you stupid Dog!
GREYMOUSE
GREAT. Now I gotta play CATCH with a BUS!
HELP, DARN IT!
You wait here, cat!
Got places to be. stuff to destroy

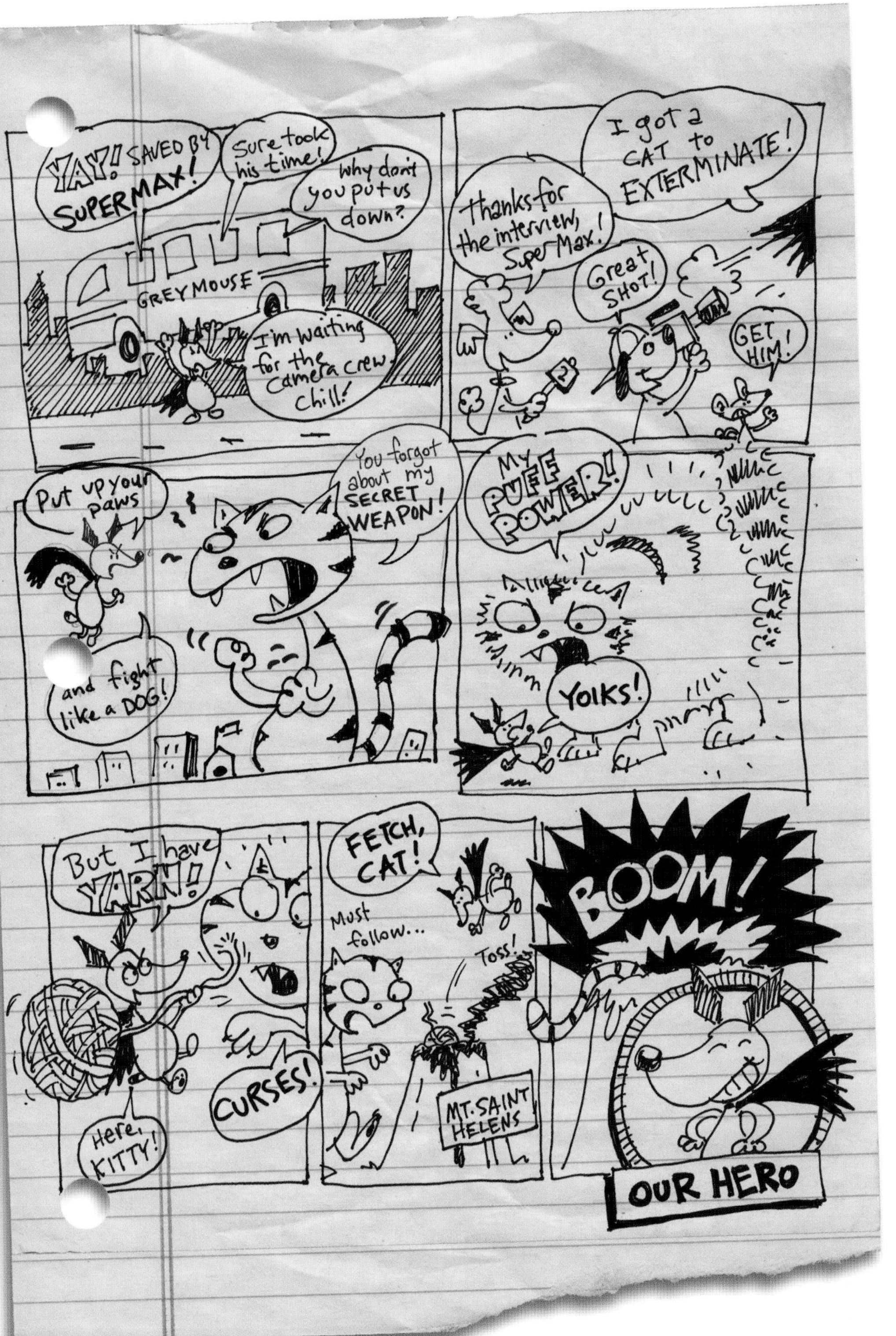
YAY! SAVED BY SUPERMAX!
Sure took his time!
Why don't you put us down?
GREYMOUSE
I'm waiting for the camera crew. Chill!
I got a CAT to EXTERMINATE!
Thanks for the interview, SuperMax!
Great SHOT!
GET HIM!
Put up your paws
and fight like a DOG!
You forgot about my SECRET WEAPON!
My PUFF POWER!
YOIKS!
But I have YARN!
Here, KITTY!
CURSES!
FETCH, CAT!
Must follow...
Toss!
MT. SAINT HELENS
BOOM!
OUR HERO

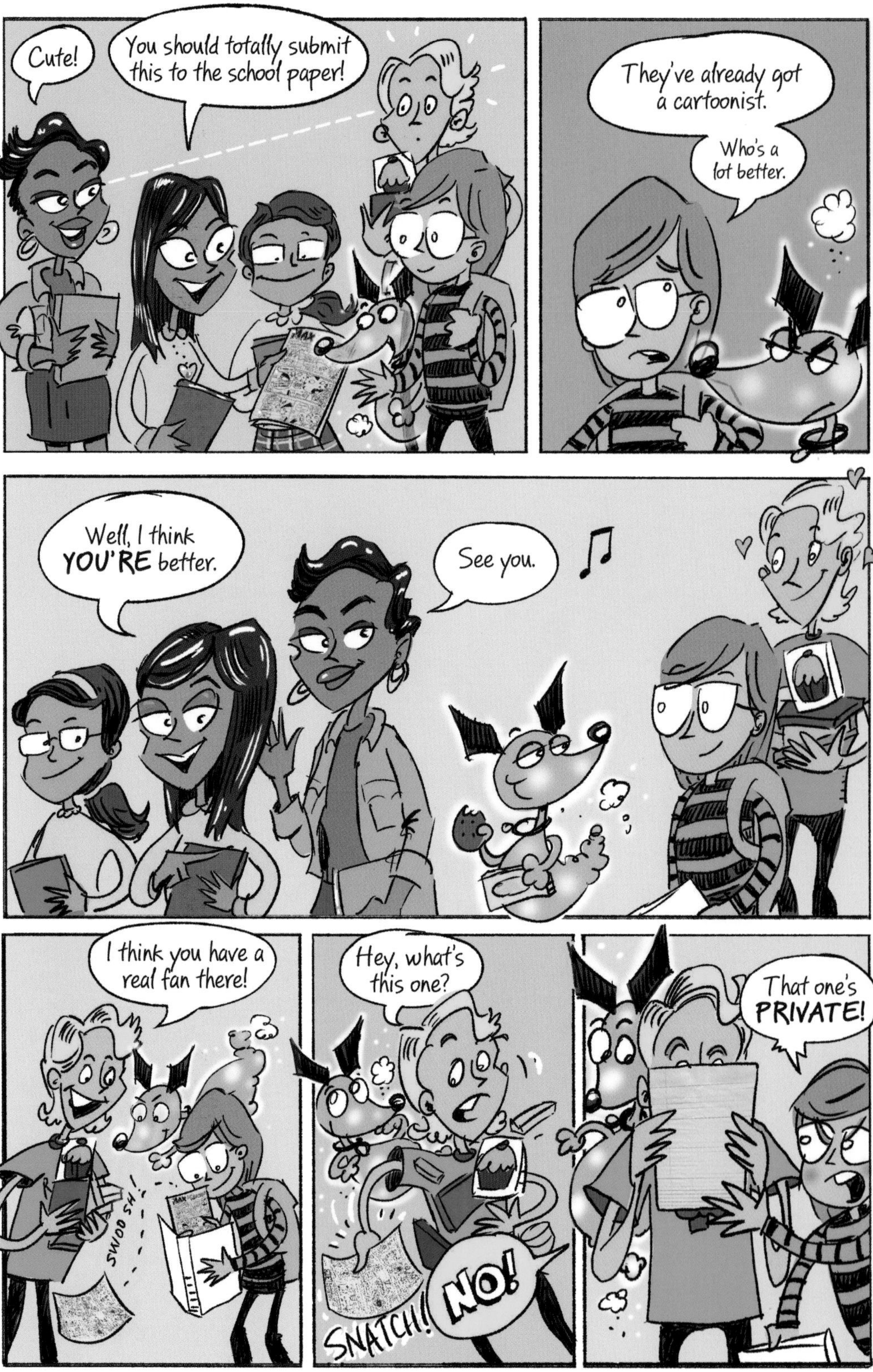
Cute!
You should totally submit this to the school paper!
They've already got a cartoonist.
Who's a lot better.
Well, I think YOU'RE better.
See you.
I think you have a real fan there!
SWOOSH!
Hey, what's this one?
SNATCH!
NO!
That one's PRIVATE!

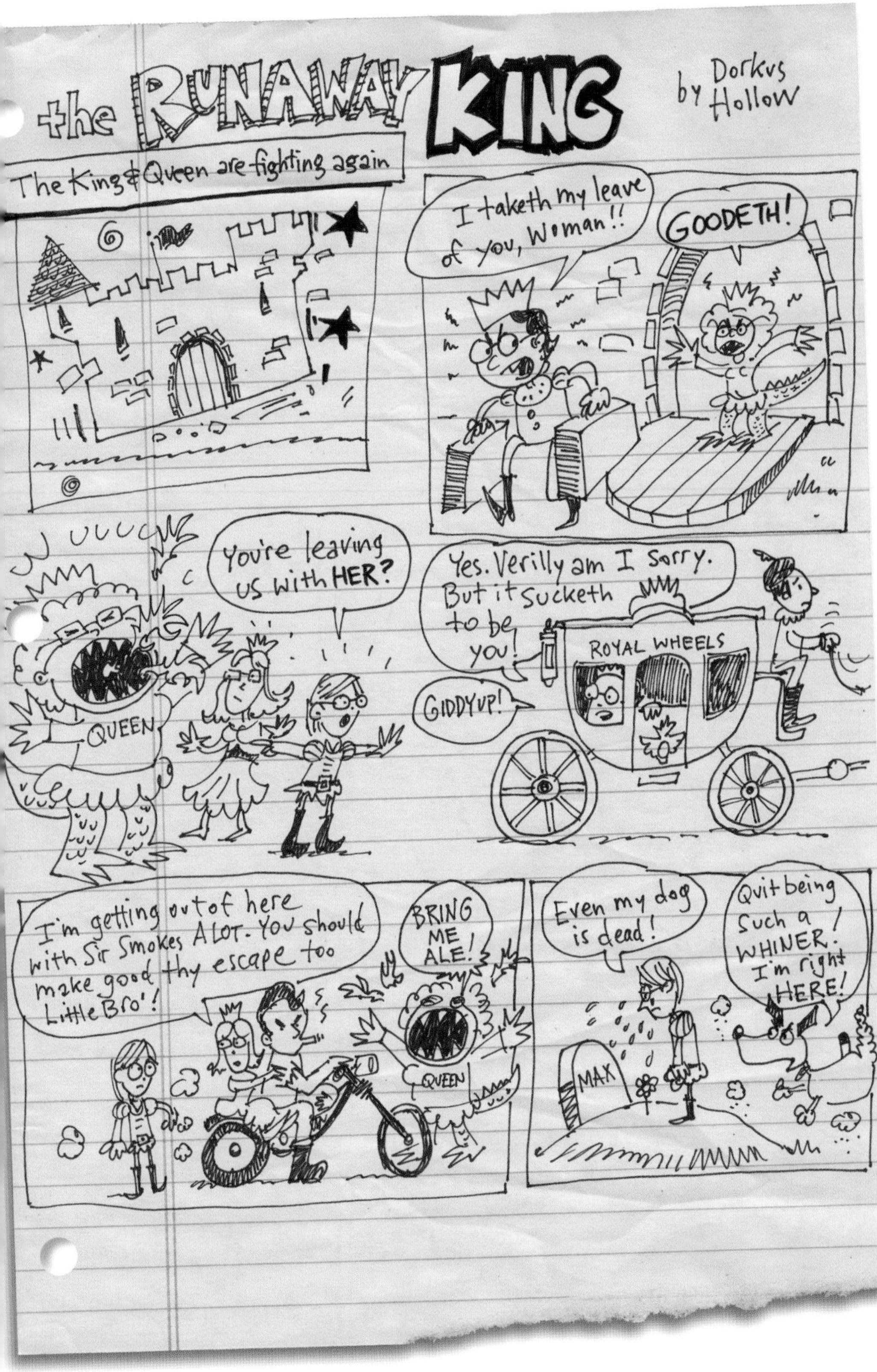
the RUNAWAY KING
by Dorkus Hollow
The King & Queen are fighting again
I taketh my leave of you, Woman!!
GOODETH!
You're leaving us with HER?
QUEEN
Yes. Verilly am I sorry. But it sucketh to be you!
ROYAL WHEELS
GIDDYUP!
I'm getting out of here with Sir Smokes A Lot. You should make good thy escape too Little Bro'!
BRING ME ALE!
QUEEN
Even my dog is dead!
MAX
Quit being such a WHINER! I'm right HERE!

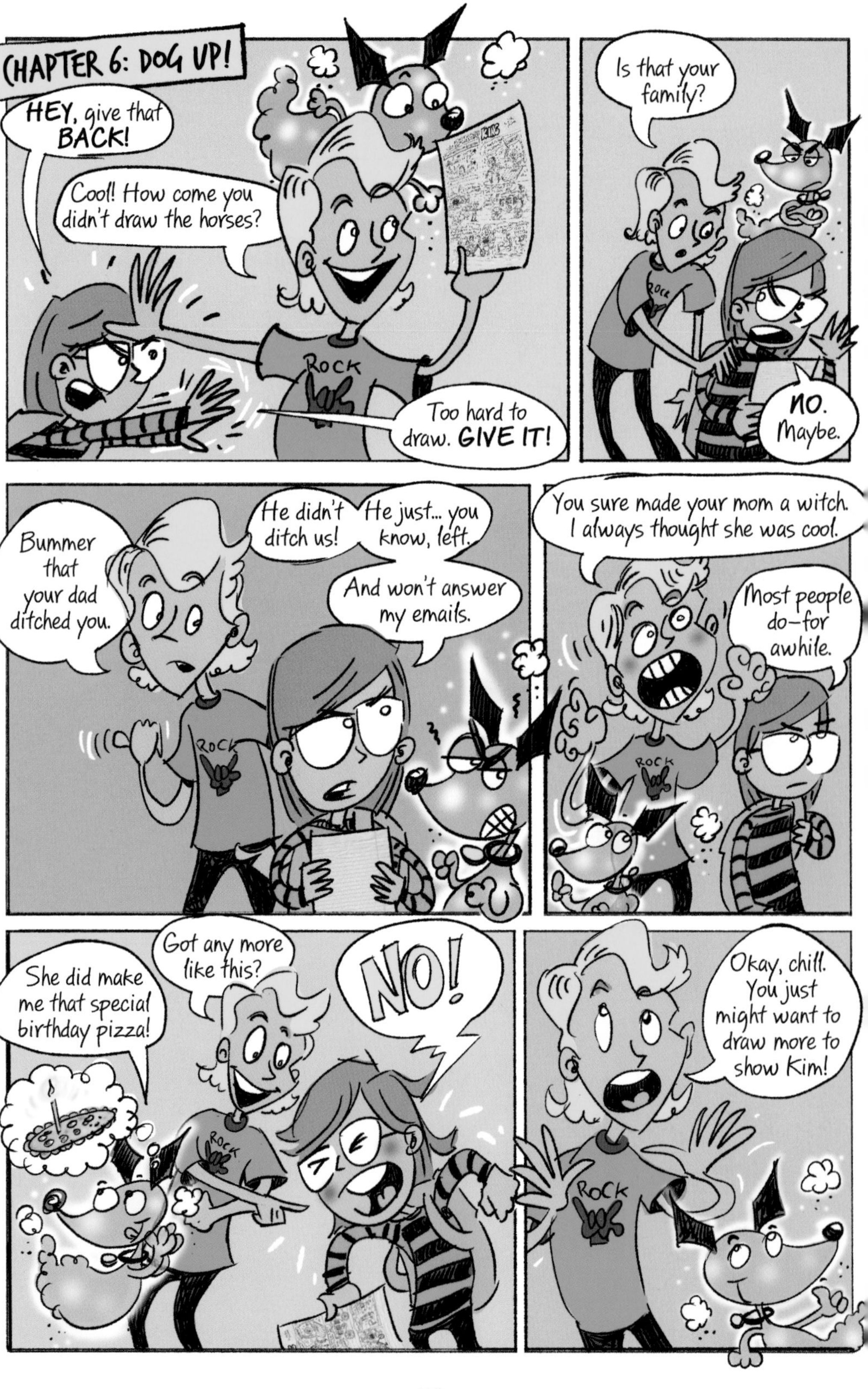
CHAPTER 6: DOG UP!
HEY, give that BACK!
Cool! How come you didn't draw the horses?
Too hard to draw. GIVE IT!
Is that your family?
NO. Maybe.
Bummer that your dad ditched you.
He didn't ditch us!
He just... you know, left.
And won't answer my emails.
You sure made your mom a witch. I always thought she was cool.
Most people do—for awhile.
She did make me that special birthday pizza!
Got any more like this?
NO!
Okay, chill. You just might want to draw more to show Kim!

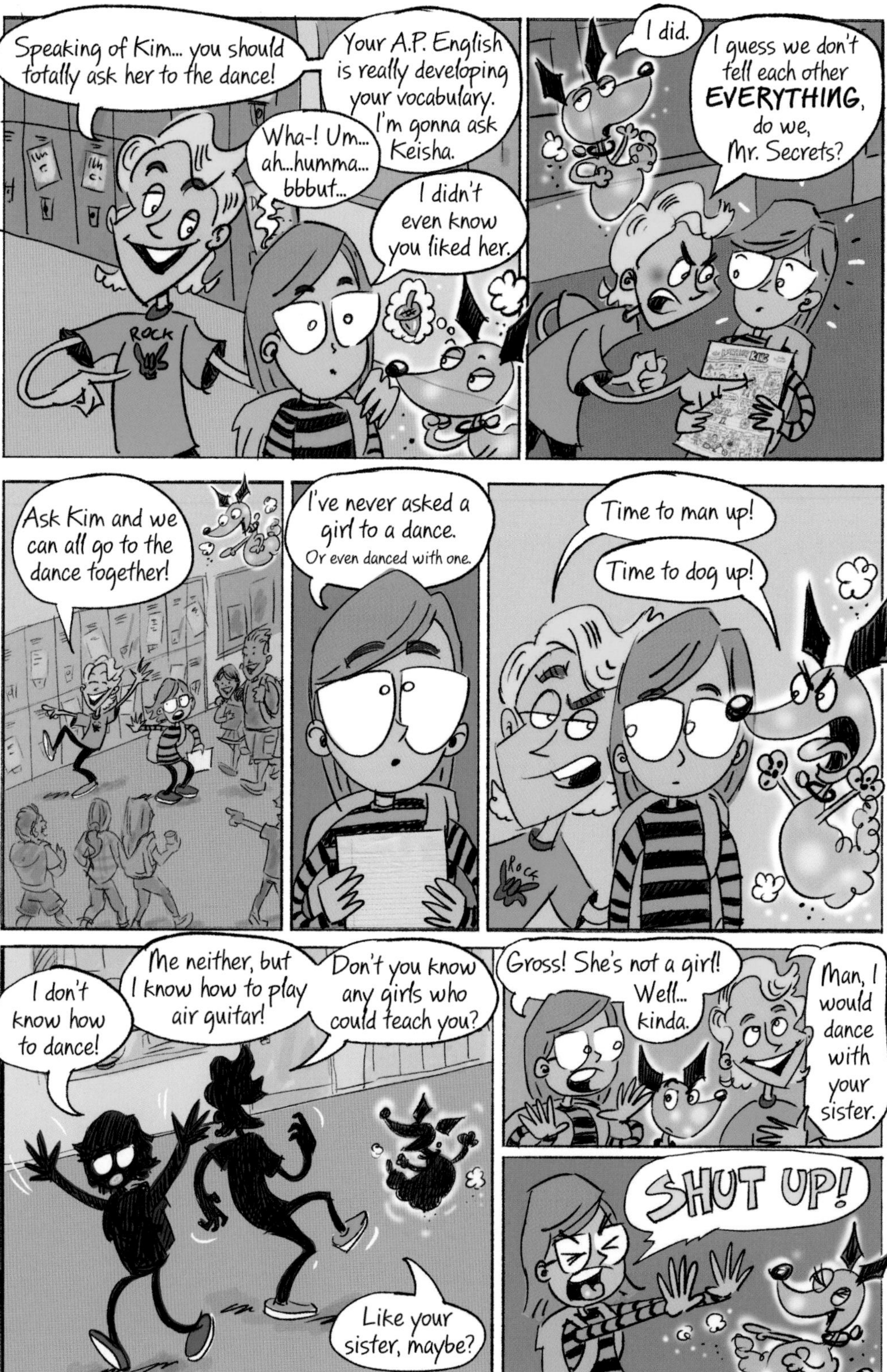
Speaking of Kim... you should totally ask her to the dance!
Wha-! Um... ah...humma... bbbut...
Your A.P. English is really developing your vocabulary. I'm gonna ask Keisha.
I didn't even know you liked her.
I did.
I guess we don't tell each other EVERYTHING, do we, Mr. Secrets?
Ask Kim and we can all go to the dance together!
I've never asked a girl to a dance. Or even danced with one.
Time to man up!
Time to dog up!
I don't know how to dance!
Me neither, but I know how to play air guitar!
Don't you know any girls who could teach you?
Like your sister, maybe?
Gross! She's not a girl! Well... kinda.
Man, I would dance with your sister.
SHUT UP!

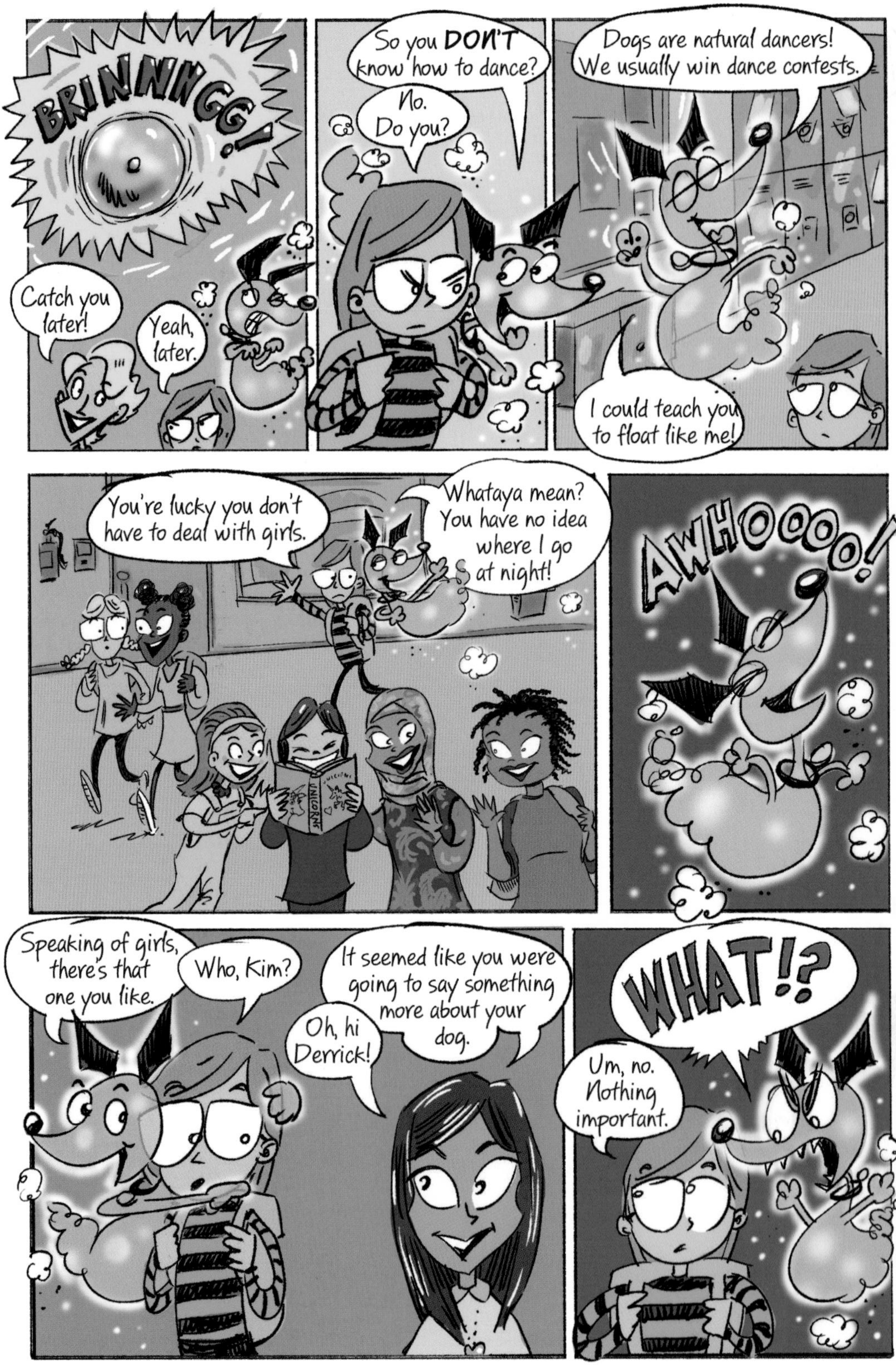
BRINNNGG!
Catch you later!
Yeah, later.
So you DON'T know how to dance?
No. Do you?
Dogs are natural dancers! We usually win dance contests.
I could teach you to float like me!
You're lucky you don't have to deal with girls.
Whataya mean? You have no idea where I go at night!
UNICORNS
AWHOOOO!
Speaking of girls, there's that one you like.
Who, Kim?
Oh, hi Derrick!
It seemed like you were going to say something more about your dog.
WHAT!?
Um, no. Nothing important.

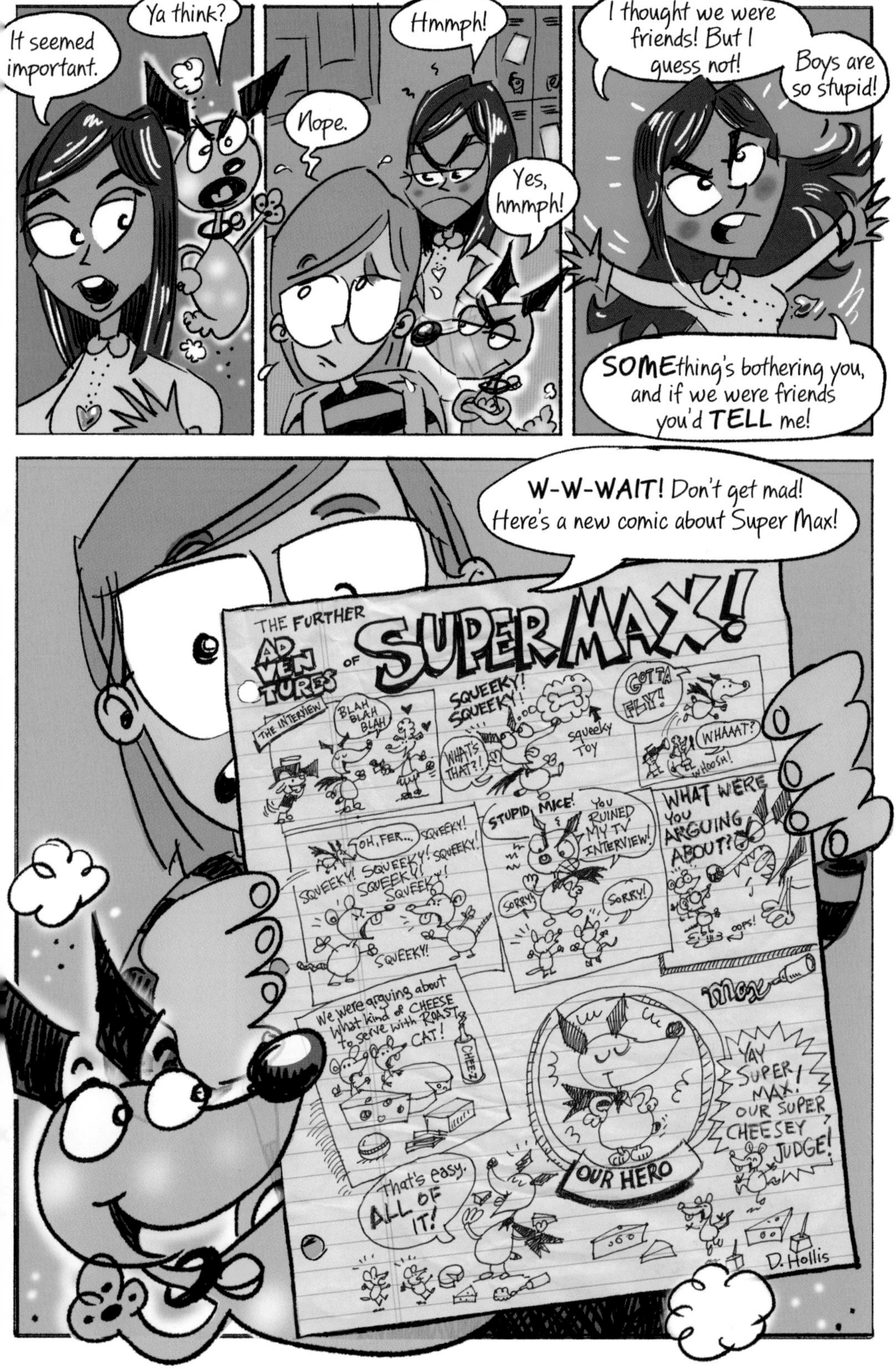
It seemed important.
Ya think?
Hmmph!
Nope.
Yes, hmmph!
I thought we were friends! But I guess not!
Boys are so stupid!
SOMEthing's bothering you, and if we were friends you'd TELL me!
W-W-WAIT! Don't get mad! Here's a new comic about Super Max!
THE FURTHER ADVENTURES OF SUPER MAX!
THE INTERVIEW
BLAH BLAH BLAH
SQUEEKY SQUEEKY!
WHAT'S THAT?!
squeeky toy
GOTTA FLY!
WHAAAT?
WHOOSH!
OH, FER...
SQUEEKY! SQUEEKY! SQUEEKY! SQUEEKY! SQUEEKY! SQUEEKY!
SQUEEKY!
STUPID MICE!
YOU RUINED MY TV INTERVIEW!
SORRY!
SORRY!
WHAT WERE YOU ARGUING ABOUT?!
OOPS!
We were arguing about what kind of CHEESE to serve with ROAST CAT!
CHEEZ
OUR HERO
YAY SUPER MAX! OUR SUPER CHEESEY JUDGE!
That's easy. ALL OF IT!
Max
D. Hollis

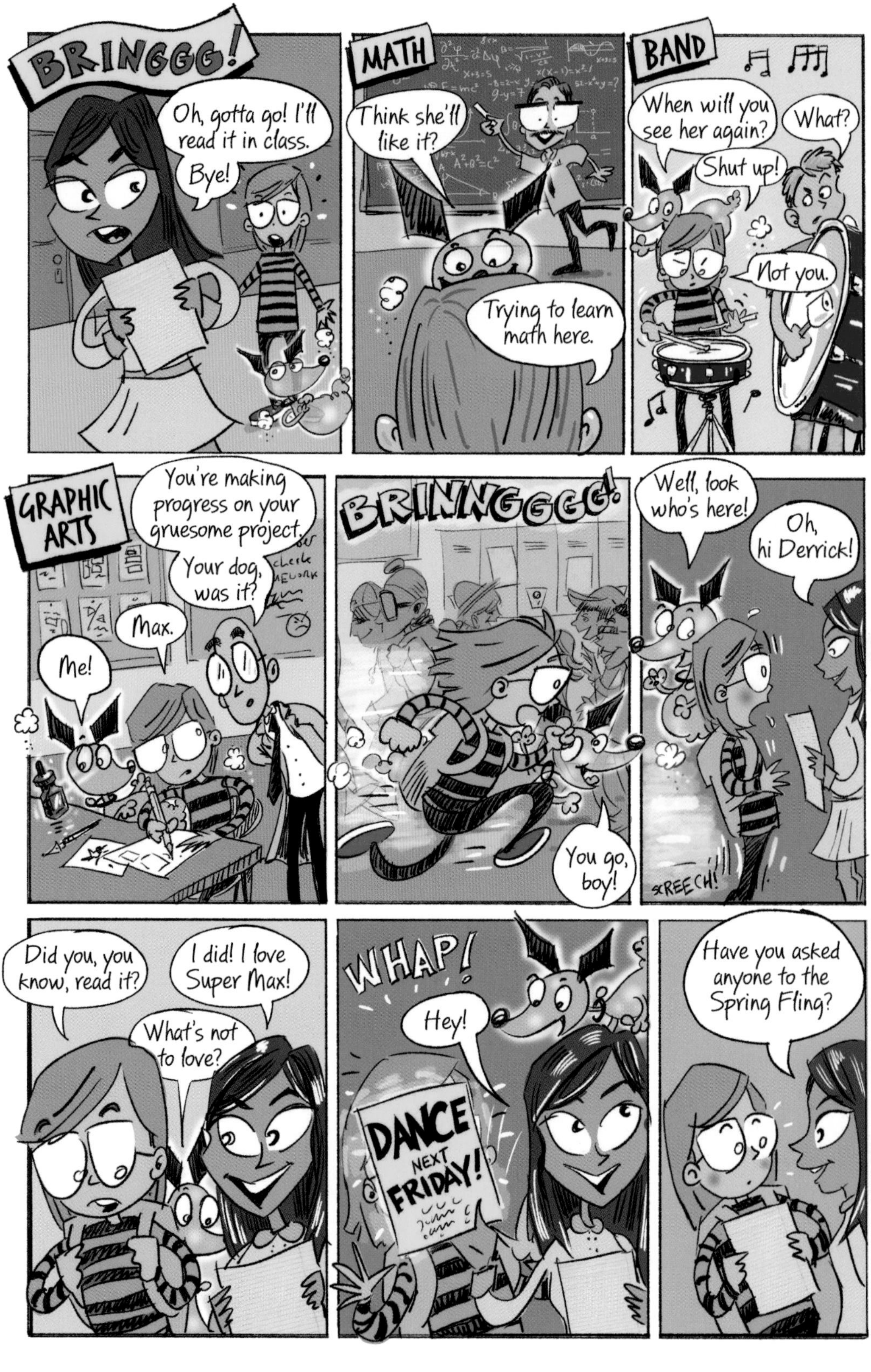
BRINGGG!
Oh, gotta go! I'll read it in class.
Bye!
MATH
Think she'll like it?
Trying to learn math here.
BAND
When will you see her again?
What?
Shut up!
Not you.
GRAPHIC ARTS
You're making progress on your gruesome project.
Your dog, was it?
Max.
Me!
BRINNGGGG!
You go, boy!
Well, look who's here!
Oh, hi Derrick!
SCREECH!
Did you, you know, read it?
I did! I love Super Max!
What's not to love?
WHAP!
Hey!
DANCE NEXT FRIDAY!
Have you asked anyone to the Spring Fling?

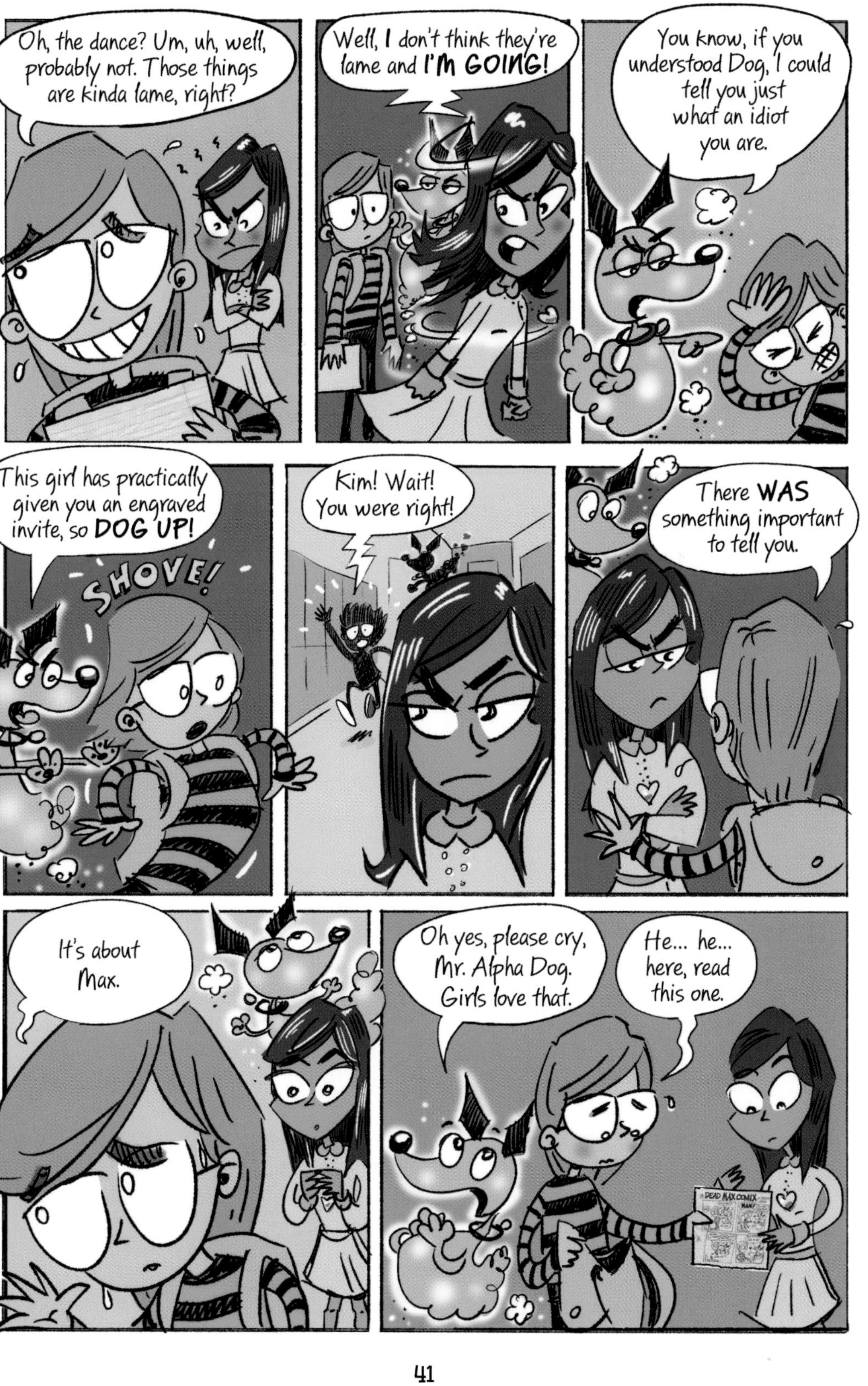

Oh, the dance? Um, uh, well, probably not. Those things are kinda lame, right?
Well, I don't think they're lame and I'M GOING!
You know, if you understood Dog, I could tell you just what an idiot you are.
This girl has practically given you an engraved invite, so DOG UP!
SHOVE!
Kim! Wait! You were right!
There WAS something important to tell you.
It's about Max.
Oh yes, please cry, Mr. Alpha Dog. Girls love that.
He... he... here, read this one.
DEAD MAX COMIX

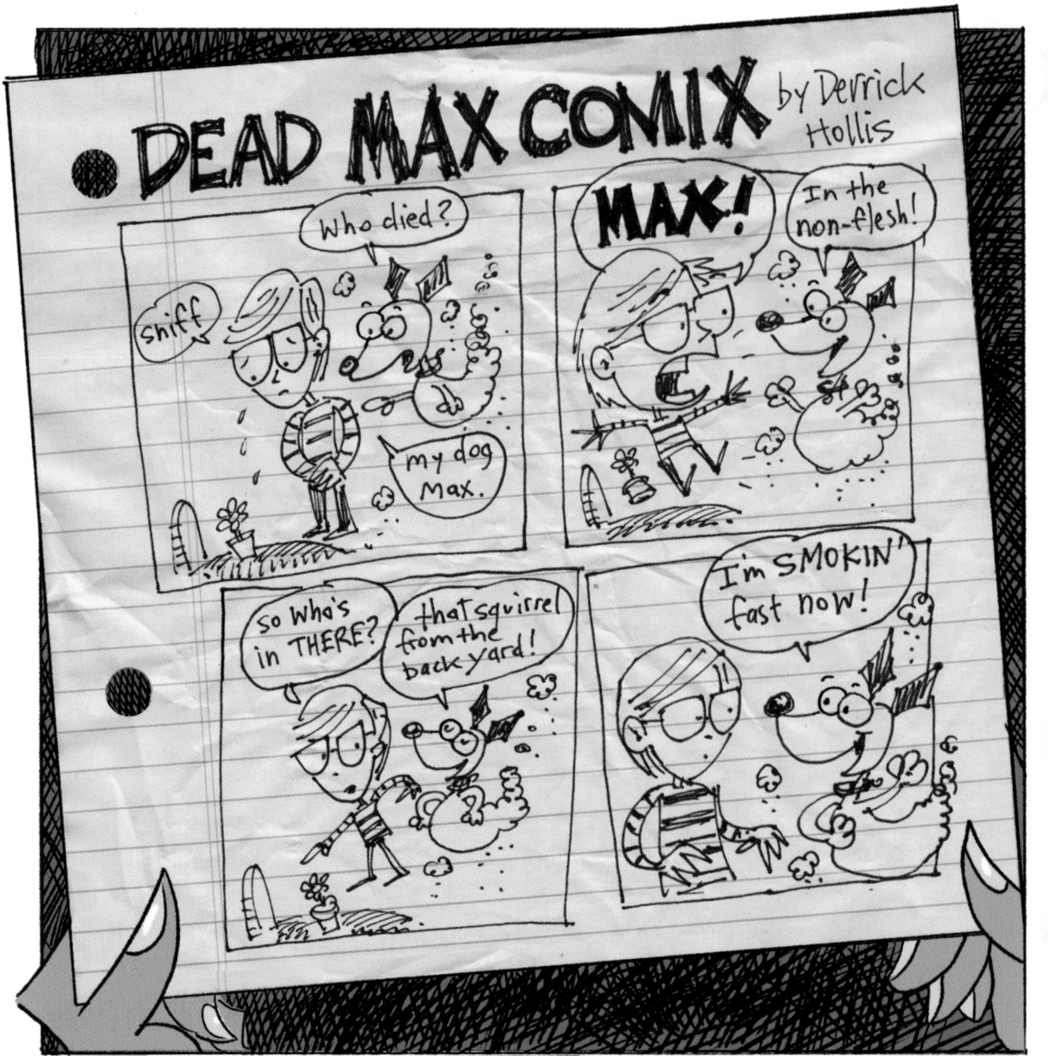
DEAD MAX COMIX by Derrick Hollis
Who died?
sniff
my dog Max.
MAX!
In the non-flesh!
So who's in THERE?
that squirrel from the back yard!
I'm SMOKIN' fast now!

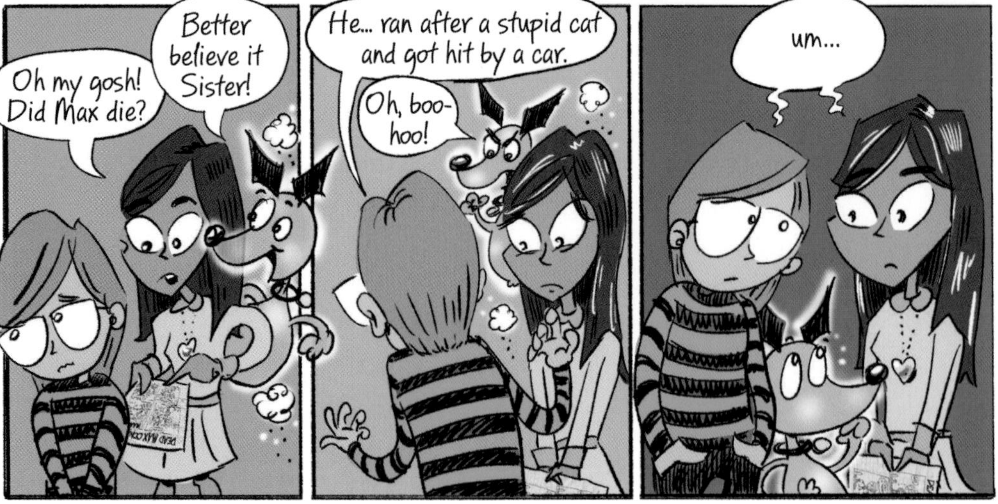
Oh my gosh! Did Max die?
Better believe it Sister!
He... ran after a stupid cat and got hit by a car.
Oh, boo-hoo!
um...

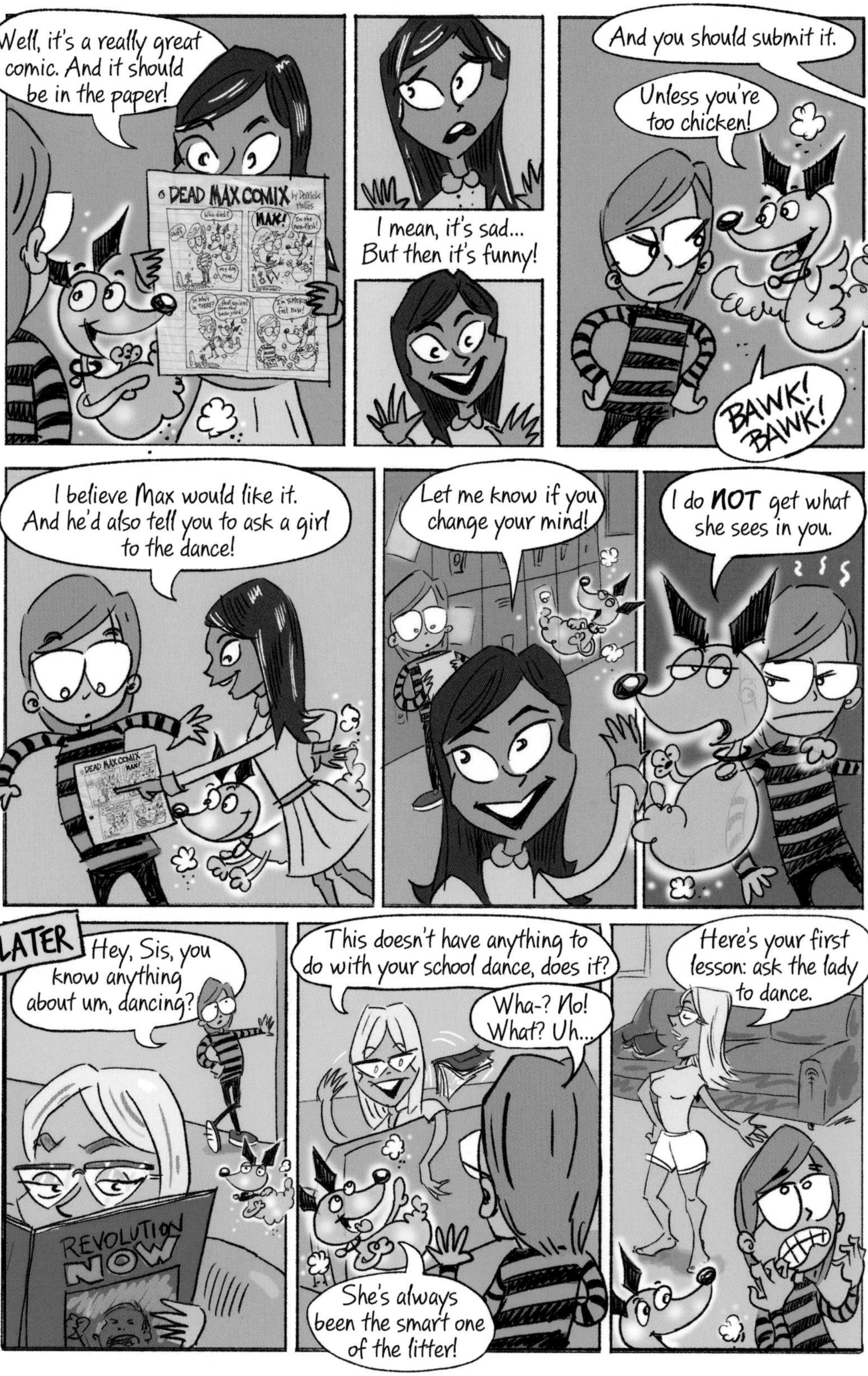
Well, it's a really great comic. And it should be in the paper!
DEAD MAX COMIX
I mean, it's sad... But then it's funny!
And you should submit it.
Unless you're too chicken!
BAWK! BAWK!
I believe Max would like it. And he'd also tell you to ask a girl to the dance!
DEAD MAX COMIX
Let me know if you change your mind!
I do NOT get what she sees in you.
LATER
Hey, Sis, you know anything about um, dancing?
REVOLUTION NOW
This doesn't have anything to do with your school dance, does it?
Wha-? No! What? Uh...
She's always been the smart one of the litter!
Here's your first lesson: ask the lady to dance.

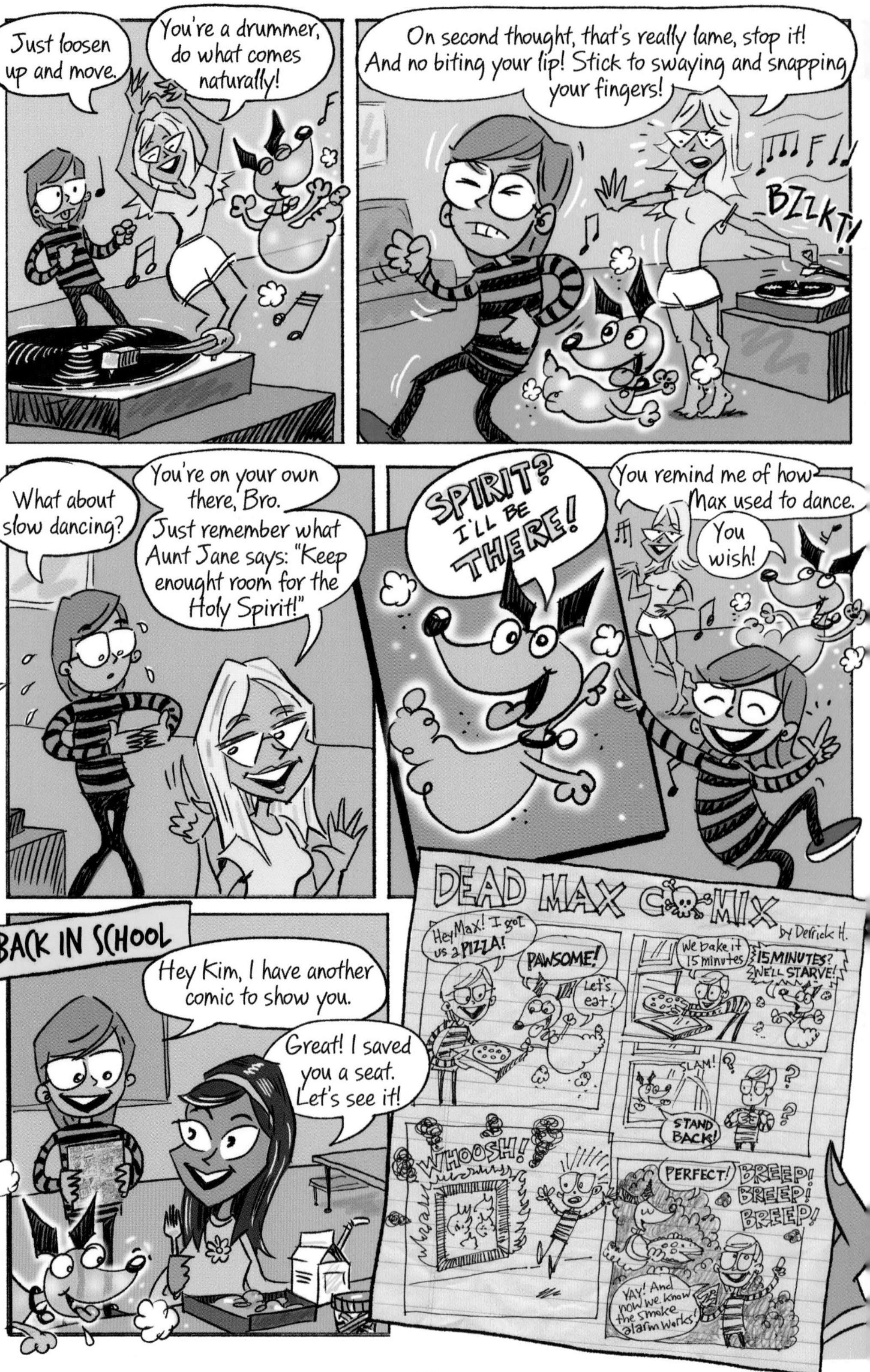

Just loosen up and move.
You're a drummer, do what comes naturally!
On second thought, that's really lame, stop it! And no biting your lip! Stick to swaying and snapping your fingers!
BZZKT!
What about slow dancing?
You're on your own there, Bro. Just remember what Aunt Jane says: "Keep enought room for the Holy Spirit!"
SPIRIT? I'LL BE THERE!
You remind me of how Max used to dance.
You wish!
BACK IN SCHOOL
Hey Kim, I have another comic to show you.
Great! I saved you a seat. Let's see it!
DEAD MAX COMIX
by Derrick H.
Hey Max! I got us a PIZZA!
PAWSOME!
Let's eat!
We bake it 15 minutes
15 MINUTES? WE'LL STARVE!
SLAM!
STAND BACK!
WHOOSH!
PERFECT!
BREEP! BREEP! BREEP!
YAY! And now we know the smoke alarm works!

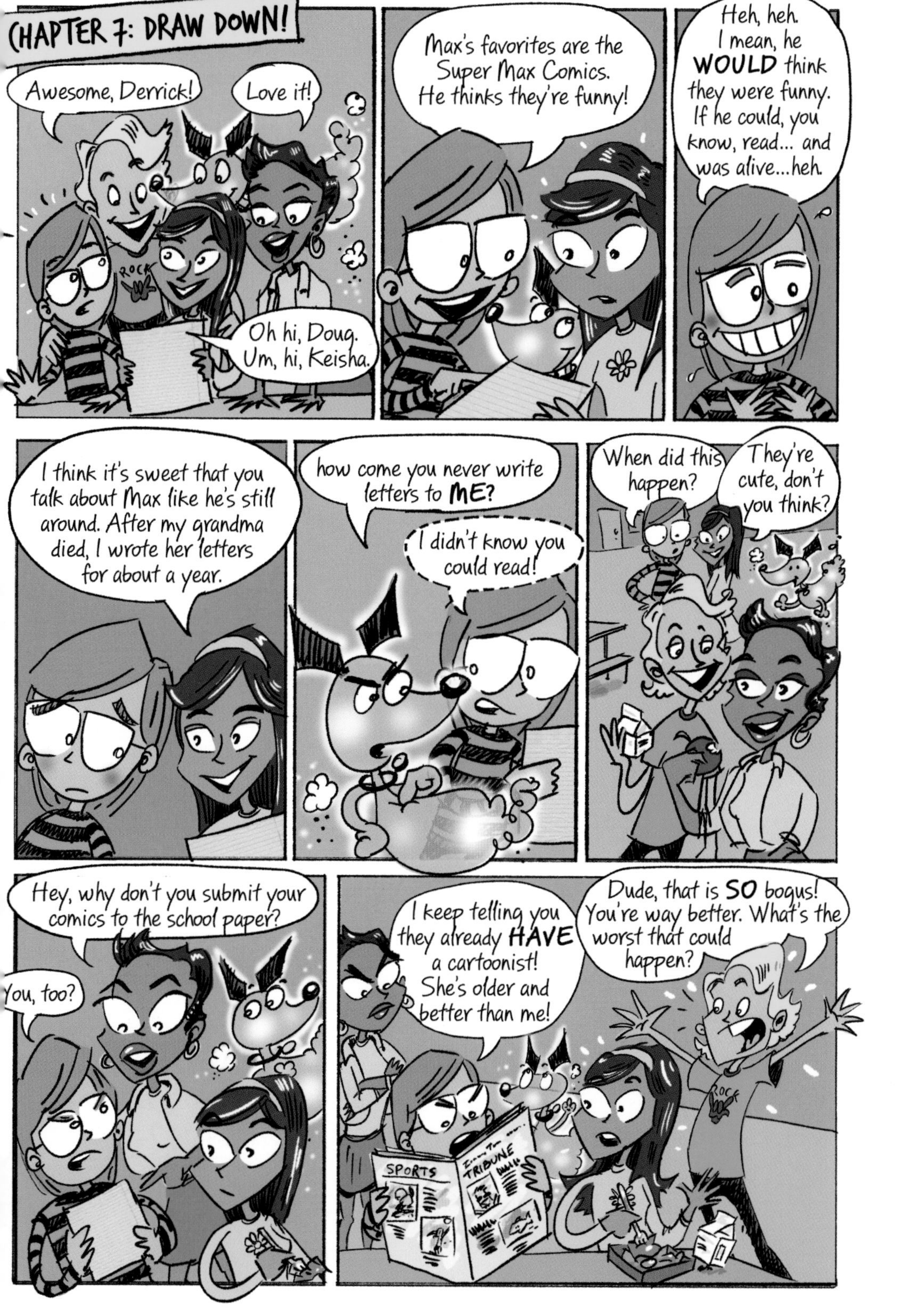

CHAPTER 7: DRAW DOWN!
Awesome, Derrick!
Love it!
Oh hi, Doug. Um, hi, Keisha.
Max's favorites are the Super Max Comics. He thinks they're funny!
Heh, heh. I mean, he WOULD think they were funny. If he could, you know, read... and was alive...heh.
I think it's sweet that you talk about Max like he's still around. After my grandma died, I wrote her letters for about a year.
how come you never write letters to ME?
I didn't know you could read!
When did this happen?
They're cute, don't you think?
Hey, why don't you submit your comics to the school paper?
You, too?
I keep telling you they already HAVE a cartoonist! She's older and better than me!
Dude, that is SO bogus! You're way better. What's the worst that could happen?
SPORTS
TRIBUNE
ROCK

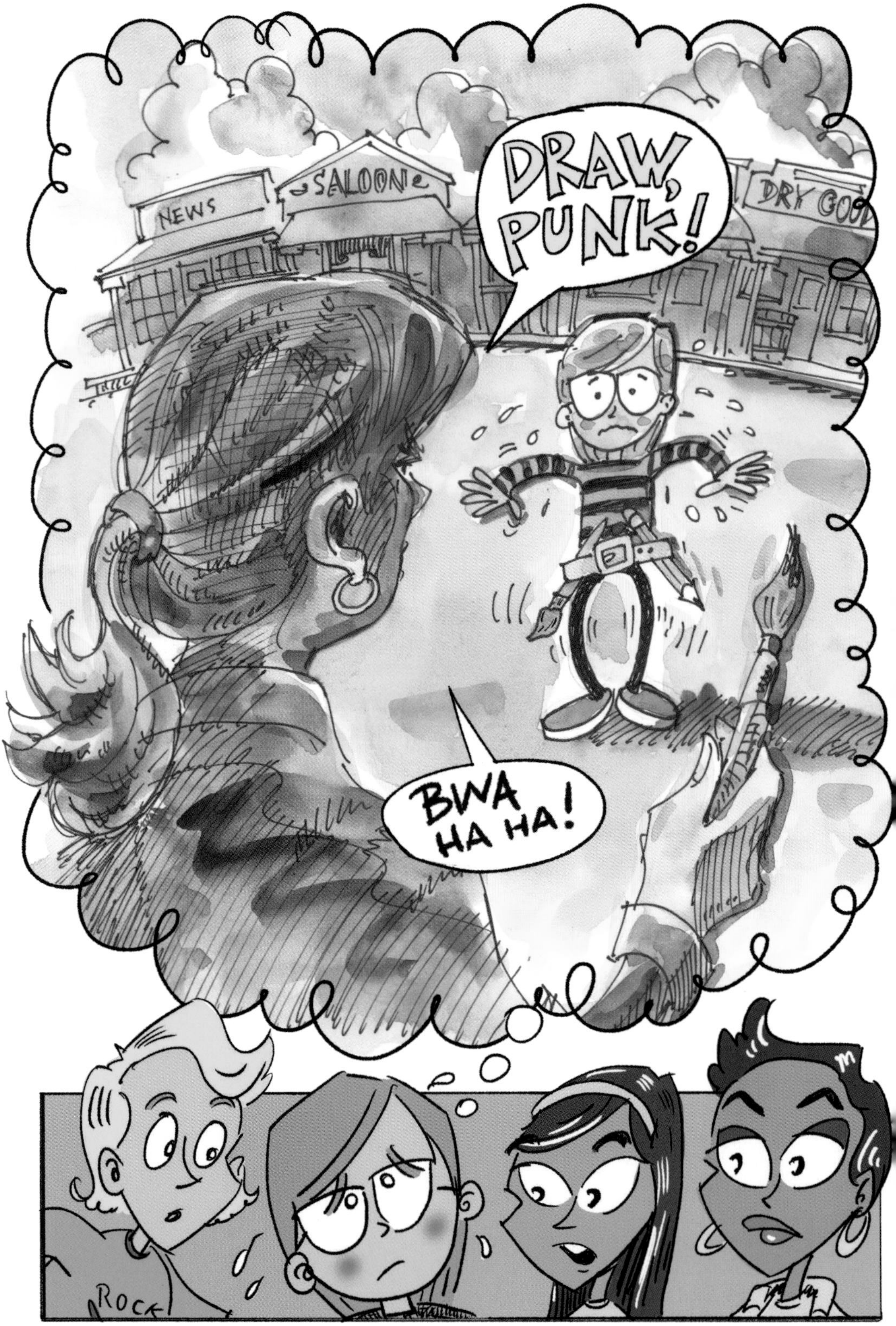
NEWS
SALOON
DRY GOOD
DRAW, PUNK!
BWA HA HA!
ROCK

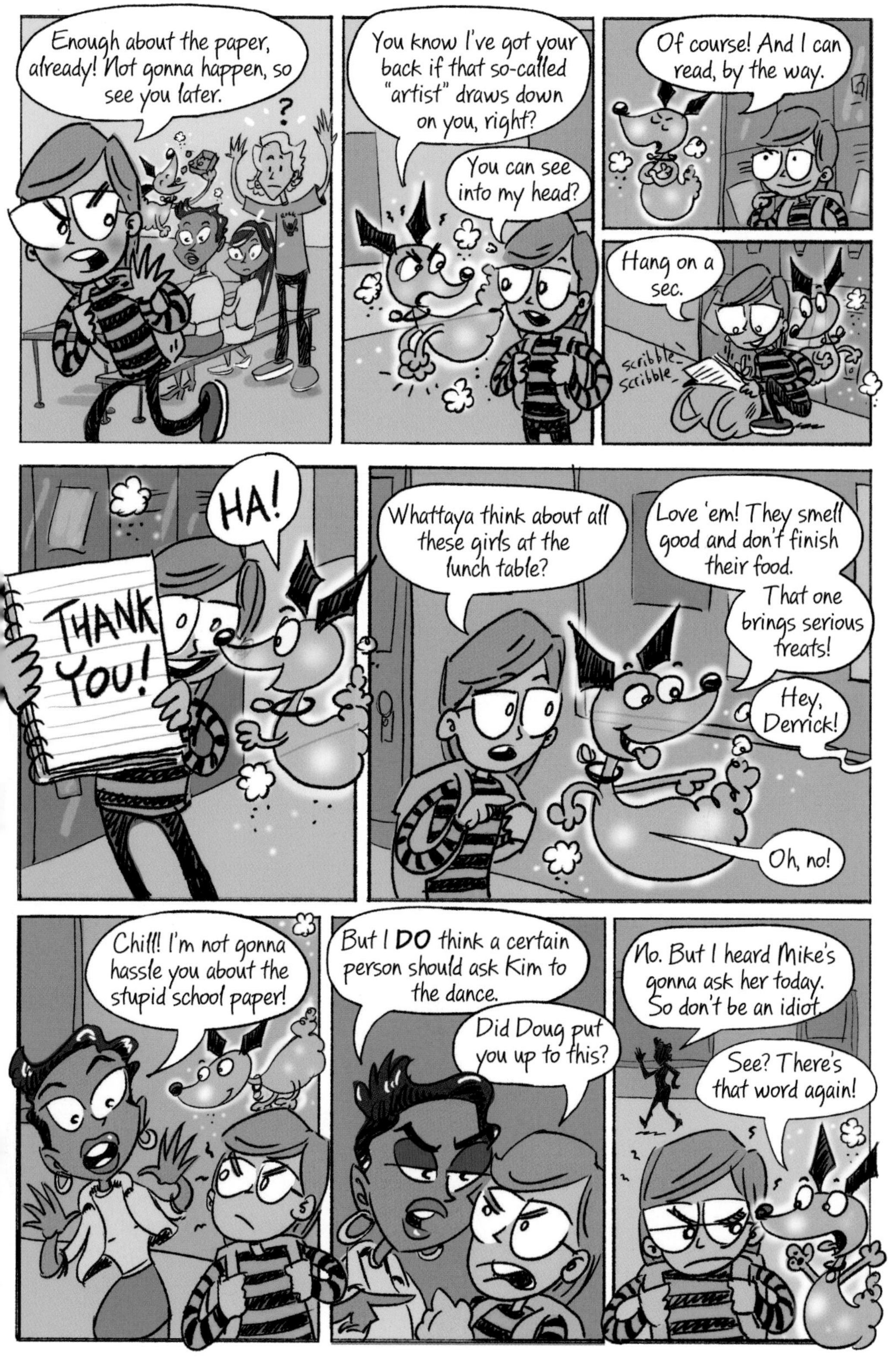

Enough about the paper, already! Not gonna happen, so see you later.
?
You know I've got your back if that so-called "artist" draws down on you, right?
You can see into my head?
Of course! And I can read, by the way.
Hang on a sec.
scribble scribble
THANK YOU!
HA!
Whattaya think about all these girls at the lunch table?
Love 'em! They smell good and don't finish their food.
That one brings serious treats!
Hey, Derrick!
Oh, no!
Chill! I'm not gonna hassle you about the stupid school paper!
But I DO think a certain person should ask Kim to the dance.
Did Doug put you up to this?
No. But I heard Mike's gonna ask her today. So don't be an idiot.
See? There's that word again!

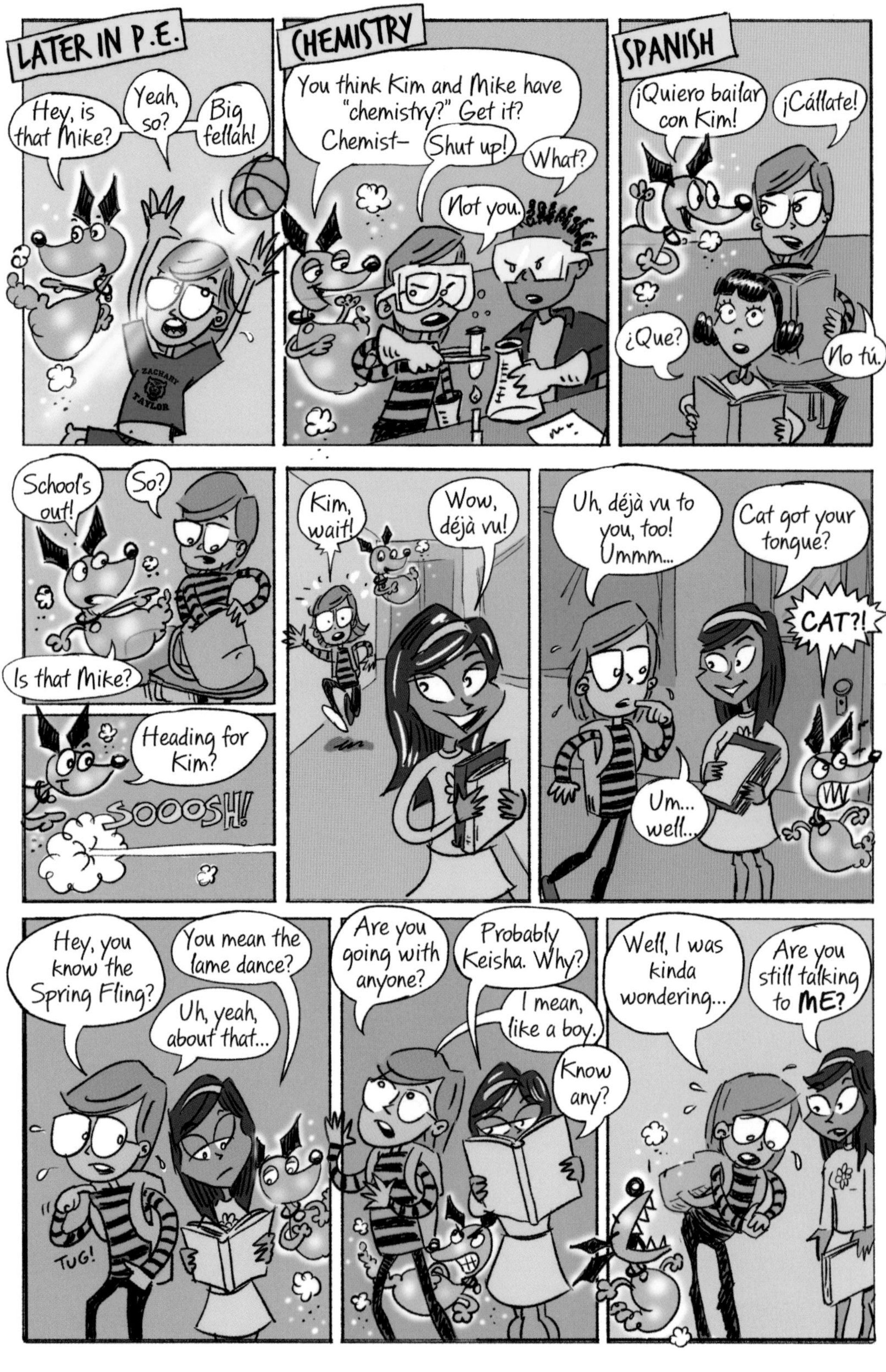
LATER IN P.E.
Hey, is that Mike?
Yeah, so?
Big fellah!
ZACHARY TAYLOR
CHEMISTRY
You think Kim and Mike have "chemistry?" Get it? Chemist–
Shut up!
What?
Not you.
SPANISH
¡Quiero bailar con Kim!
¡Cállate!
¿Que?
No tú.
School's out!
So?
Is that Mike?
Heading for Kim?
SOOOSH!
Kim, wait!
Wow, déjà vu!
Uh, déjà vu to you, too! Ummm...
Cat got your tongue?
CAT?!
Um... well...
Hey, you know the Spring Fling?
You mean the lame dance?
Uh, yeah, about that...
TUG!
Are you going with anyone?
Probably Keisha. Why?
I mean, like a boy.
Know any?
Well, I was kinda wondering...
Are you still talking to ME?

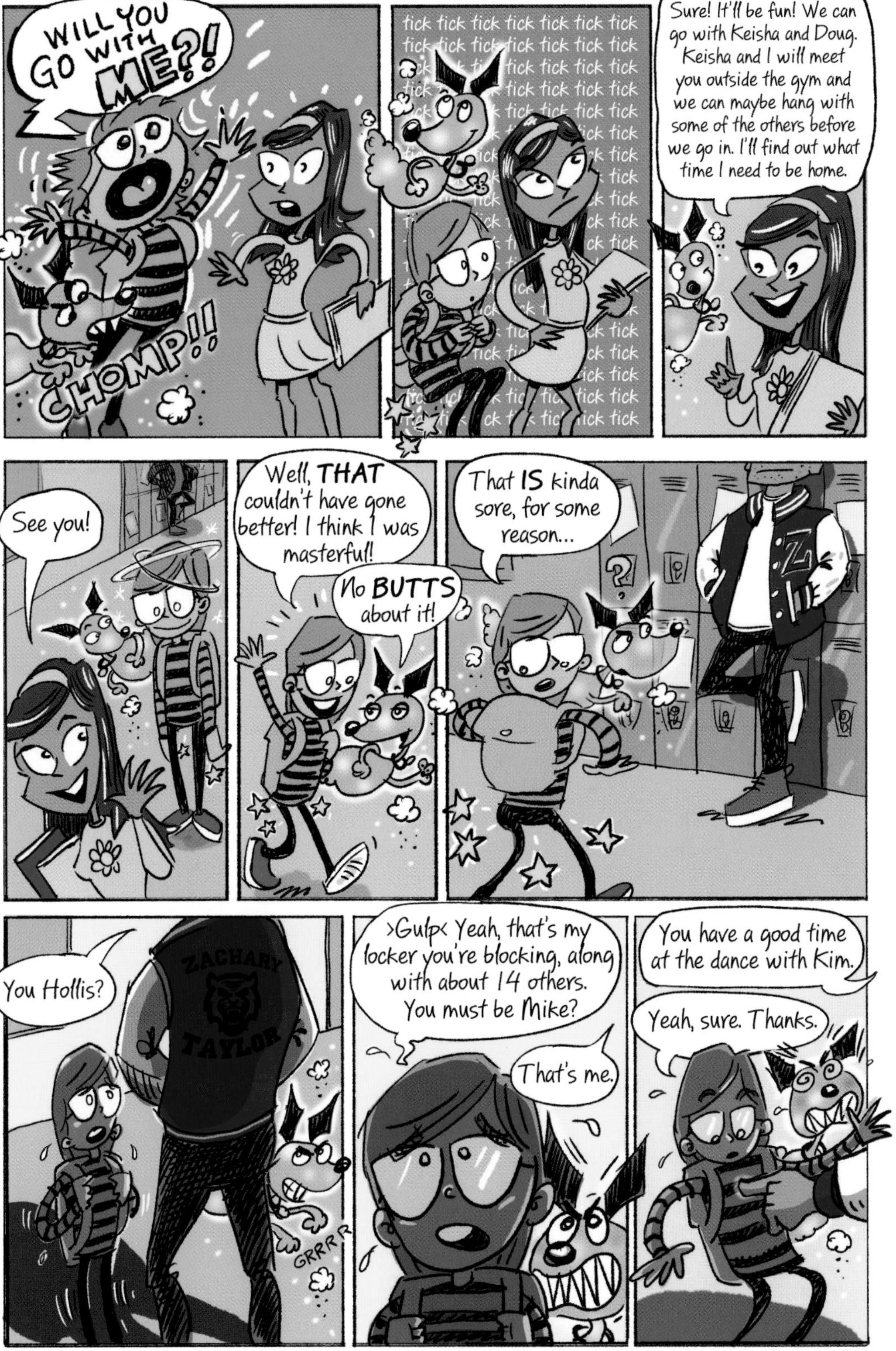
WILL YOU GO WITH ME?!
CHOMP!!
tick tick tick tick tick tick tick
Sure! It'll be fun! We can go with Keisha and Doug. Keisha and I will meet you outside the gym and we can maybe hang with some of the others before we go in. I'll find out what time I need to be home.
See you!
Well, THAT couldn't have gone better! I think I was masterful!
No BUTTS about it!
That IS kinda sore, for some reason...
?
You Hollis?
ZACHARY TAYLOR
GRRRR
>Gulp< Yeah, that's my locker you're blocking, along with about 14 others. You must be Mike?
That's me.
You have a good time at the dance with Kim.
Yeah, sure. Thanks.

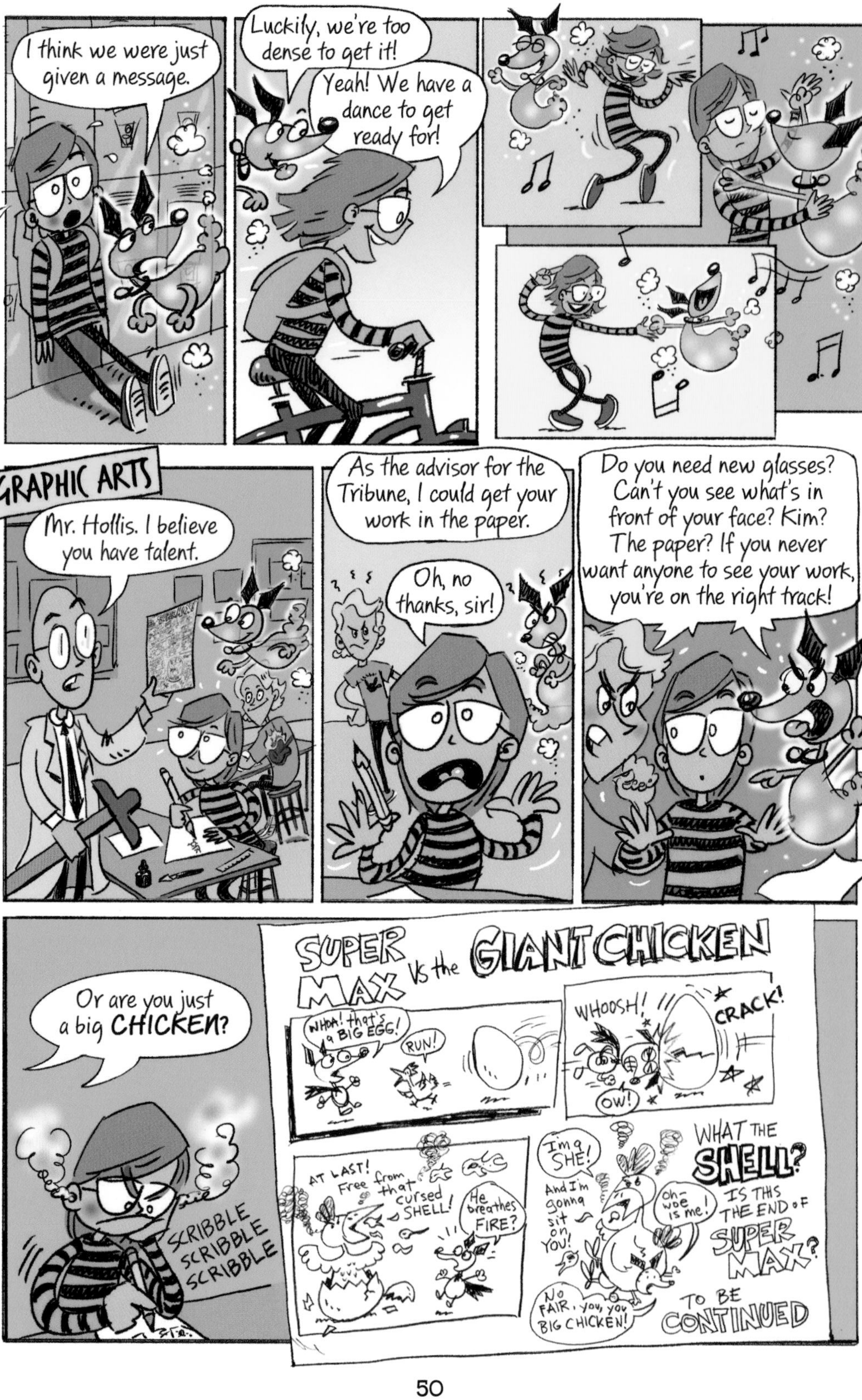
I think we were just given a message.
Luckily, we're too dense to get it!
Yeah! We have a dance to get ready for!
GRAPHIC ARTS
Mr. Hollis. I believe you have talent.
As the advisor for the Tribune, I could get your work in the paper.
Oh, no thanks, sir!
Do you need new glasses? Can't you see what's in front of your face? Kim? The paper? If you never want anyone to see your work, you're on the right track!
Or are you just a big CHICKEN?
SCRIBBLE SCRIBBLE SCRIBBLE
SUPER MAX VS the GIANT CHICKEN
WHOA! that's a BIG EGG!
RUN!
WHOOSH!
CRACK!
OW!
AT LAST! Free from that cursed SHELL!
He breathes FIRE?
I'm a SHE!
And I'm gonna sit on YOU!
Oh-woe is me!
NO FAIR, you, you BIG CHICKEN!
WHAT THE SHELL? IS THIS THE END OF SUPER MAX?
TO BE CONTINUED

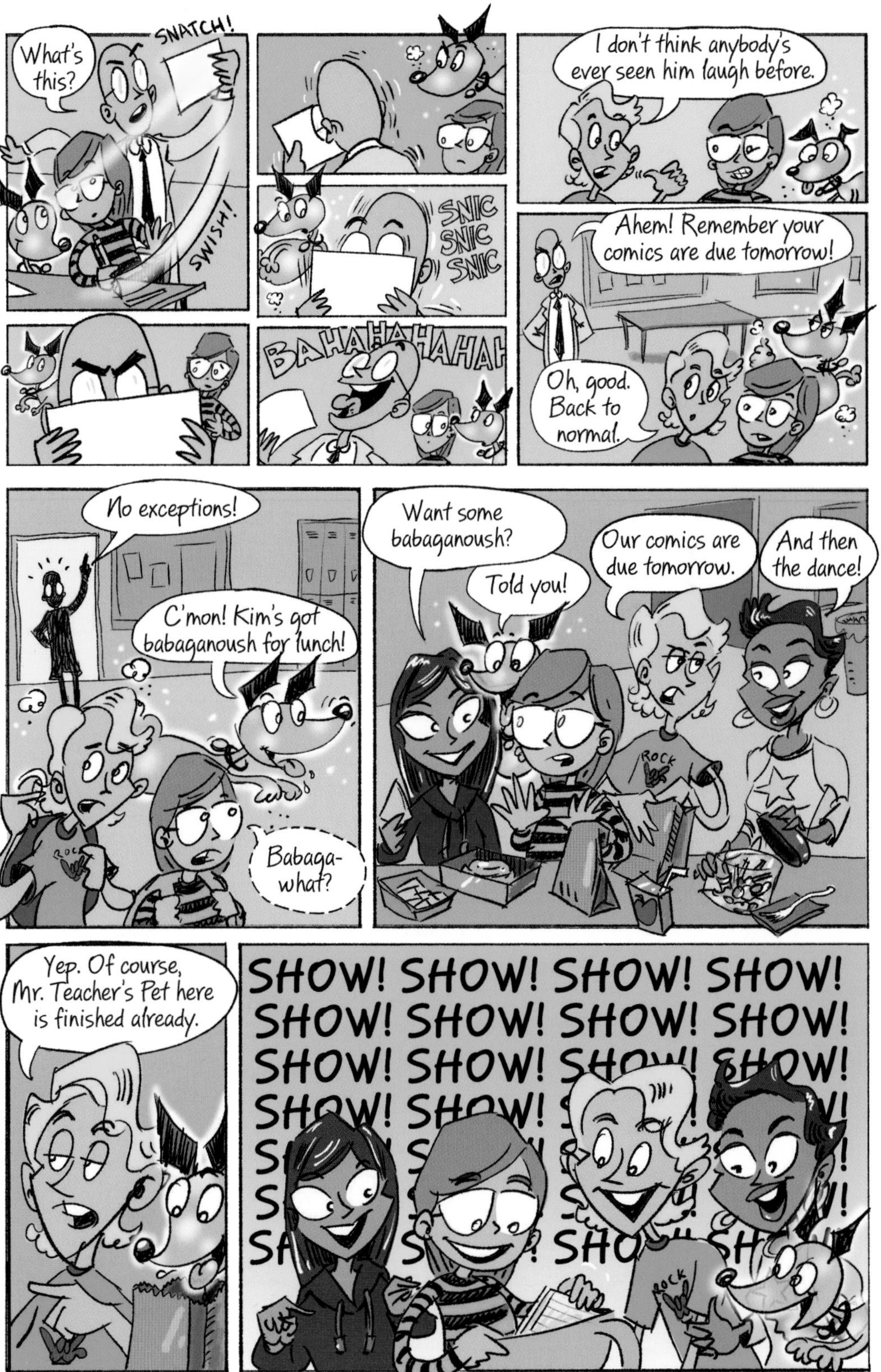
What's this?
SNATCH!
SWISH!
SNIC SNIC SNIC
BAHAHAHAHAHAH
I don't think anybody's ever seen him laugh before.
Ahem! Remember your comics are due tomorrow!
Oh, good. Back to normal.
No exceptions!
C'mon! Kim's got babaganoush for lunch!
Babaga-what?
Want some babaganoush?
Told you!
Our comics are due tomorrow.
And then the dance!
ROCK
Yep. Of course, Mr. Teacher's Pet here is finished already.
SHOW! SHOW! SHOW! SHOW!
SHOW! SHOW! SHOW! SHOW!
SHOW! SHOW!
SHOW! SHOW!

CHAPTER 8: SHAKE YOUR TAIL!

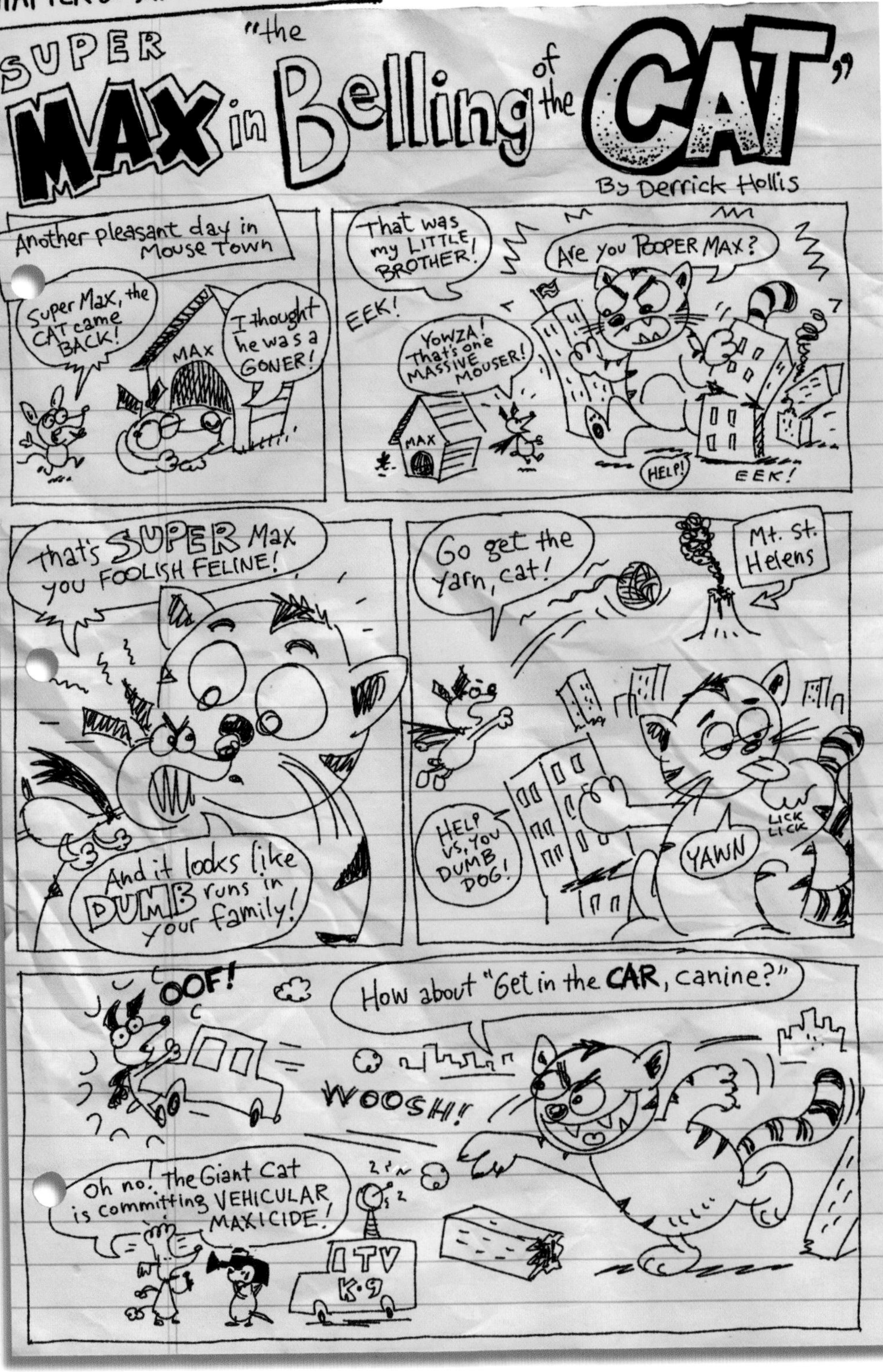

SUPER MAX in "the Belling of the CAT"
By Derrick Hollis
Another pleasant day in Mouse Town
Super Max, the CAT came BACK!
MAX
I thought he was a GONER!
That was my LITTLE BROTHER!
EEK!
Are you POOPER MAX?
YOWZA! That's one MASSIVE MOUSER!
MAX
HELP!
EEK!
that's SUPER Max you FOOLISH FELINE!
And it looks like DUMB runs in your family!
Go get the yarn, cat!
Mt. St. Helens
HELP US, YOU DUMB DOG!
YAWN
LICK LICK
OOF!
How about "Get in the CAR, canine?"
WOOSH!
Oh no! The Giant Cat is committing VEHICULAR MAXICIDE!
ITV K-9

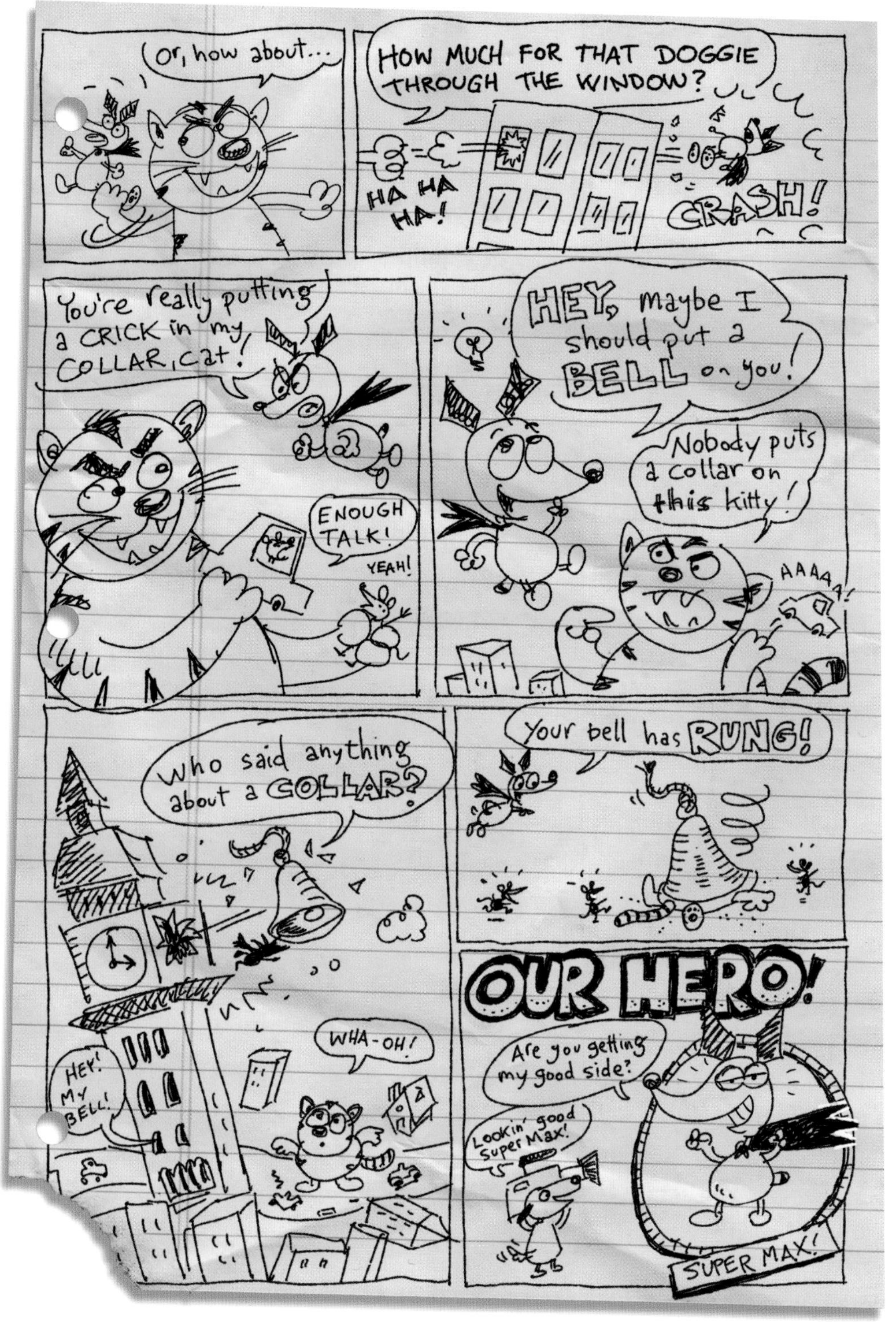
Or, how about...
HOW MUCH FOR THAT DOGGIE THROUGH THE WINDOW?
HA HA HA!
CRASH!
You're really putting a CRICK in my COLLAR, cat!
ENOUGH TALK!
YEAH!
HEY, maybe I should put a BELL on you!
Nobody puts a collar on this kitty!
AAAAA!
Who said anything about a COLLAR?
WHA-OH!
HEY! MY BELL!
Your bell has RUNG!
OUR HERO!
Are you getting my good side?
Lookin' good Super Max!
SUPER MAX!

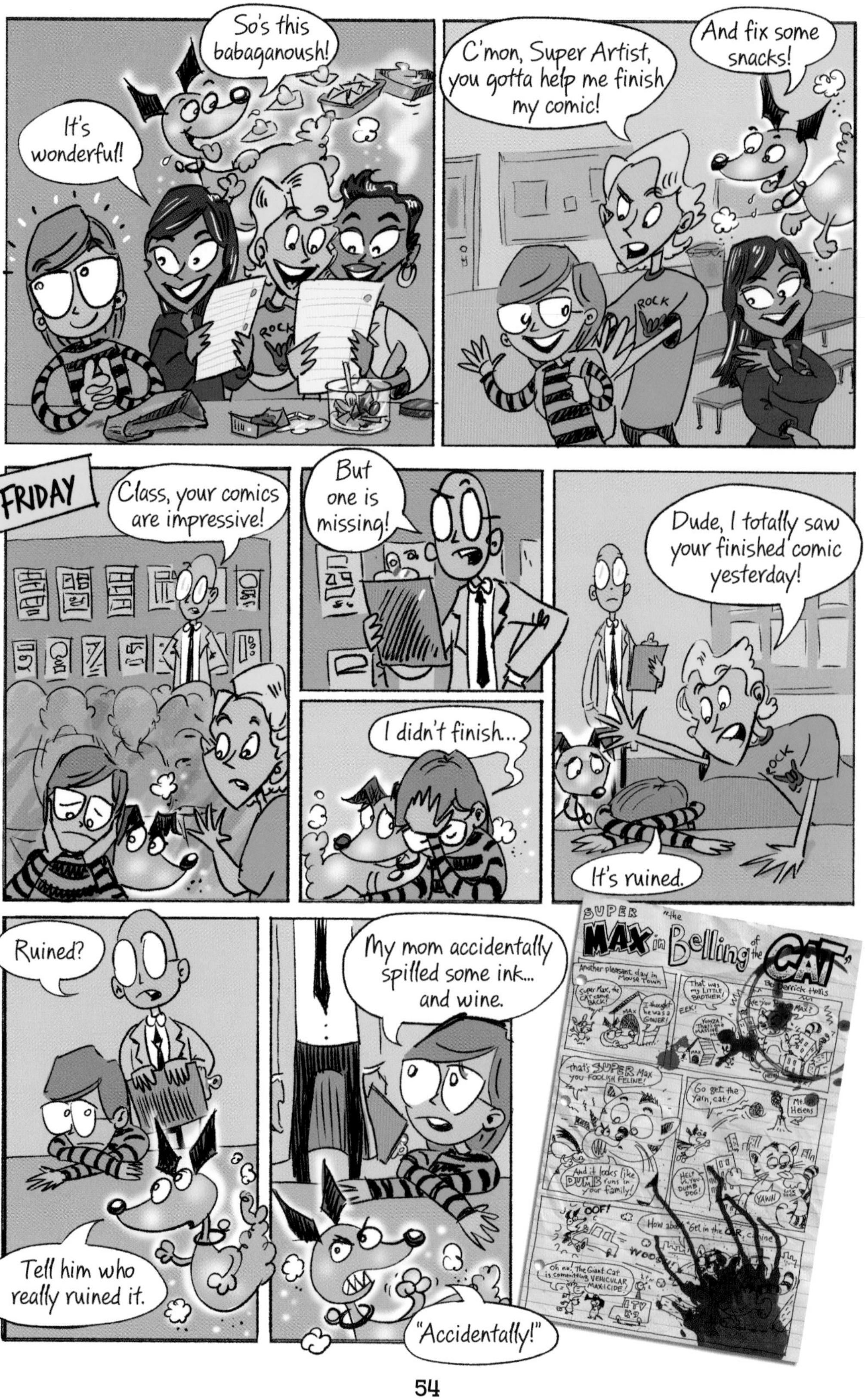
So's this babaganoush!
It's wonderful!
C'mon, Super Artist, you gotta help me finish my comic!
And fix some snacks!
FRIDAY
Class, your comics are impressive!
But one is missing!
I didn't finish...
Dude, I totally saw your finished comic yesterday!
It's ruined.
Ruined?
Tell him who really ruined it.
My mom accidentally spilled some ink... and wine.
"Accidentally!"
SUPER MAX in "the Belling of the CAT"
Another pleasant day in Mouse Town
Super Max, the CAT came BACK!
I thought he was a GONER!
That was my LITTLE BROTHER!
EEK!
that's SUPER Max you FOOLISH FELINE!
Go get the Yarn, cat!
Mt. Helens
And it looks like DUMB runs in your family!
HELP us, you DUMB DOG!
YAWN!
OOF!
Oh no! The Giant Cat is committing VEHICULAR MAXICIDE!

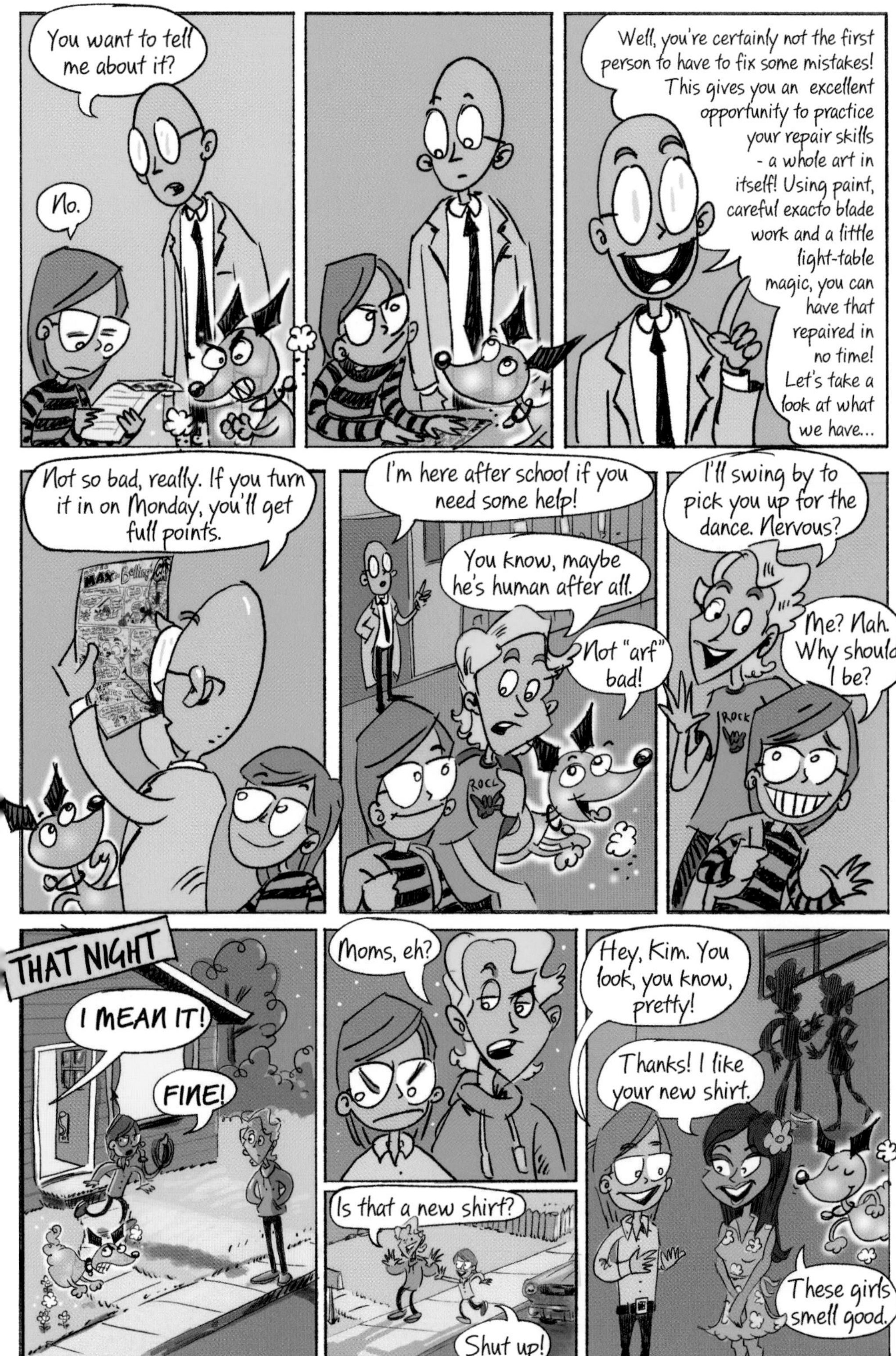
You want to tell me about it?
No.
Well, you're certainly not the first person to have to fix some mistakes! This gives you an excellent opportunity to practice your repair skills - a whole art in itself! Using paint, careful exacto blade work and a little light-table magic, you can have that repaired in no time! Let's take a look at what we have...
Not so bad, really. If you turn it in on Monday, you'll get full points.
I'm here after school if you need some help!
You know, maybe he's human after all.
Not "arf" bad!
I'll swing by to pick you up for the dance. Nervous?
Me? Nah. Why should I be?
THAT NIGHT
I MEAN IT!
FINE!
Moms, eh?
Is that a new shirt?
Shut up!
Hey, Kim. You look, you know, pretty!
Thanks! I like your new shirt.
These girls smell good.

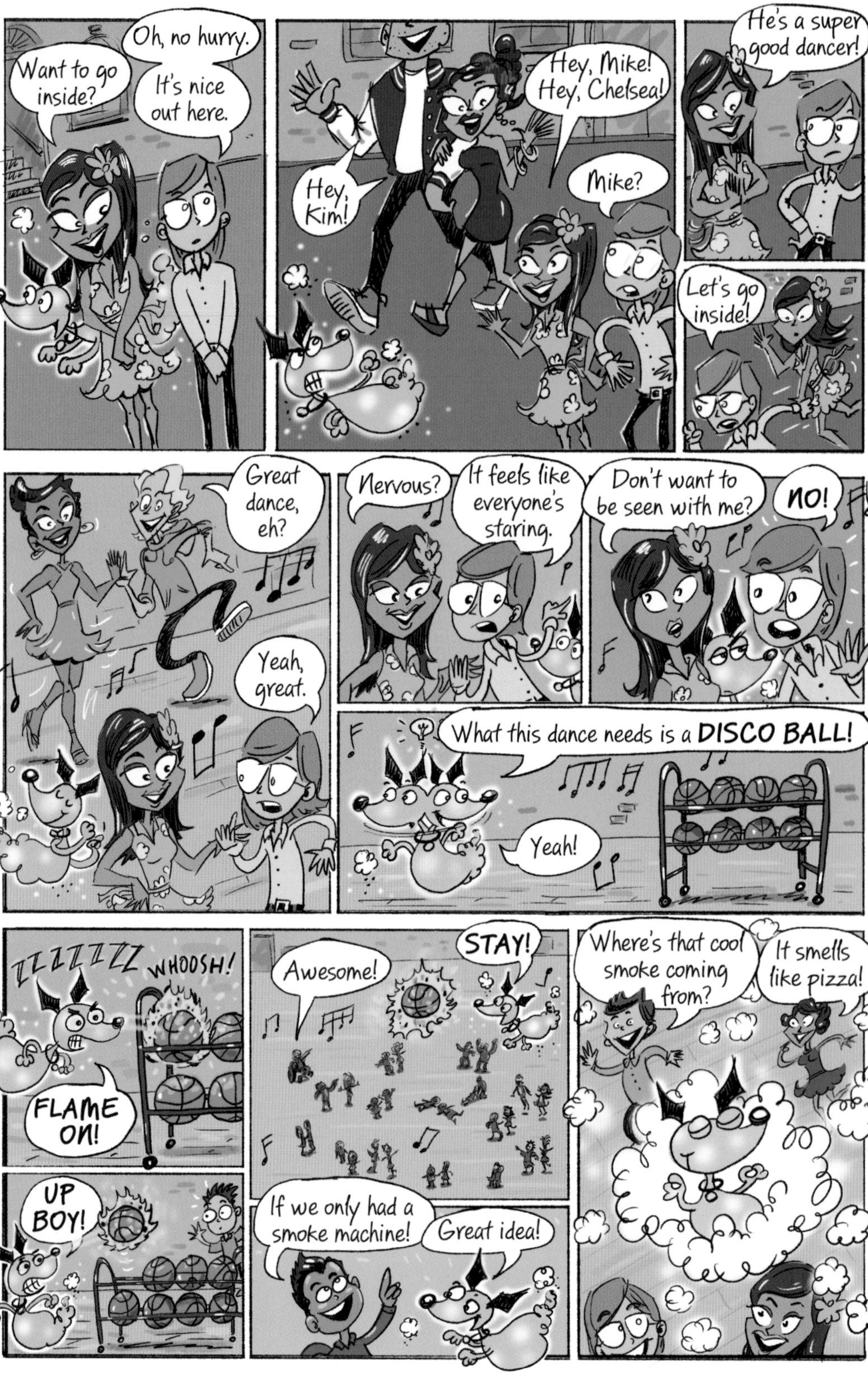
Want to go inside?
Oh, no hurry.
It's nice out here.
Hey, Mike! Hey, Chelsea!
Hey, Kim!
Mike?
He's a super good dancer!
Let's go inside!
Great dance, eh?
Yeah, great.
Nervous?
It feels like everyone's staring.
Don't want to be seen with me?
NO!
What this dance needs is a DISCO BALL!
Yeah!
ZZZZZZZ
WHOOSH!
FLAME ON!
UP BOY!
Awesome!
STAY!
If we only had a smoke machine!
Great idea!
Where's that cool smoke coming from?
It smells like pizza!

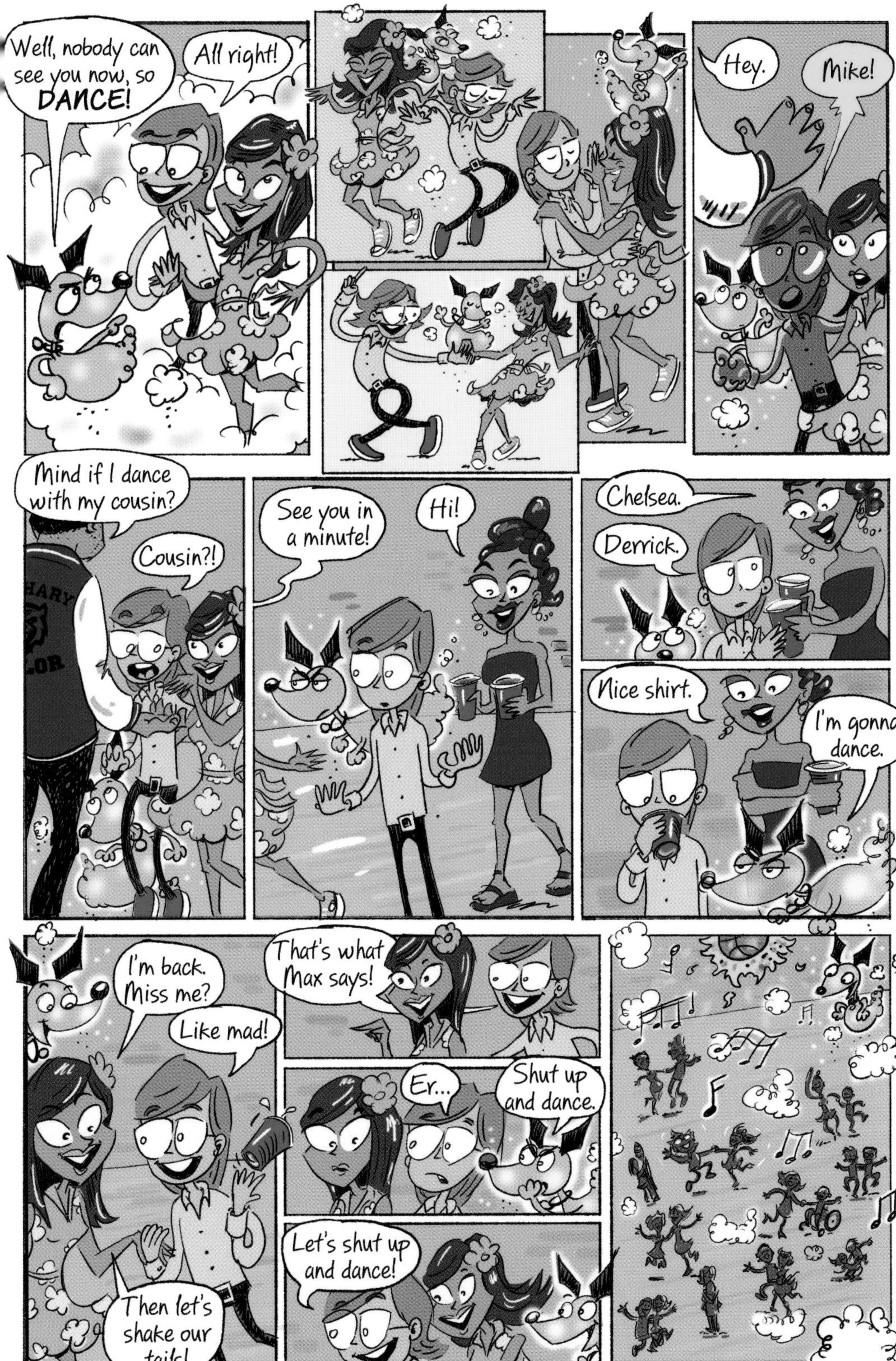

Well, nobody can see you now, so DANCE!
All right!
Hey.
Mike!
Mind if I dance with my cousin?
Cousin?!
See you in a minute!
Hi!
Chelsea.
Derrick.
Nice shirt.
I'm gonna dance.
I'm back. Miss me?
Like mad!
Then let's shake our tails!
That's what Max says!
Er...
Shut up and dance.
Let's shut up and dance!

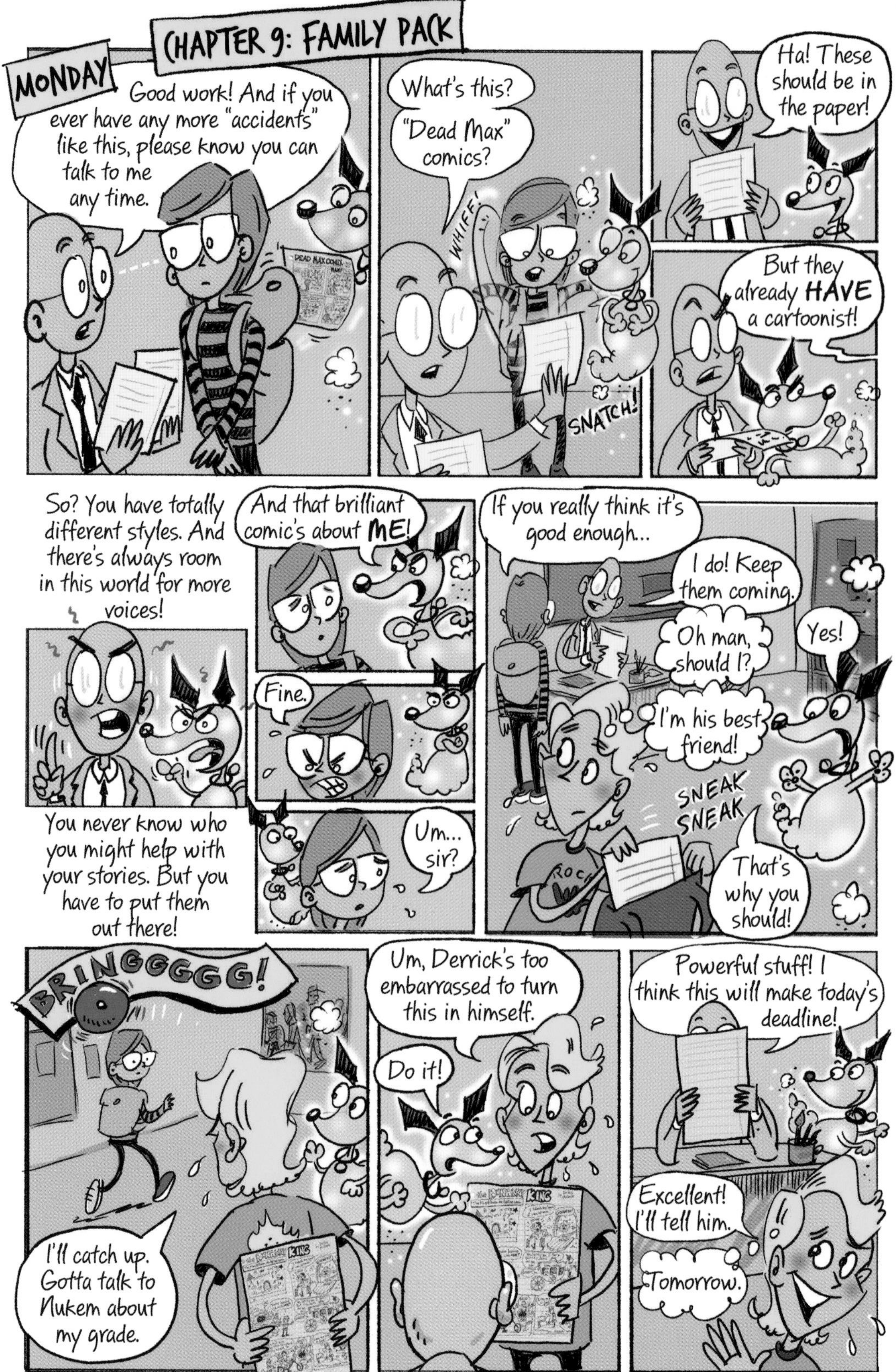
CHAPTER 9: FAMILY PACK
MONDAY
Good work! And if you ever have any more "accidents" like this, please know you can talk to me any time.
DEAD MAX COMIX
What's this?
"Dead Max" comics?
WHIFF!
SNATCH!
Ha! These should be in the paper!
But they already HAVE a cartoonist!
So? You have totally different styles. And there's always room in this world for more voices!
And that brilliant comic's about ME!
Fine.
You never know who you might help with your stories. But you have to put them out there!
Um... sir?
If you really think it's good enough...
I do! Keep them coming.
Oh man, should I?
Yes!
I'm his best friend!
SNEAK SNEAK
That's why you should!
BRINGGGGG!
I'll catch up. Gotta talk to Nukem about my grade.
Um, Derrick's too embarrassed to turn this in himself.
Do it!
Powerful stuff! I think this will make today's deadline!
Excellent! I'll tell him.
Tomorrow.

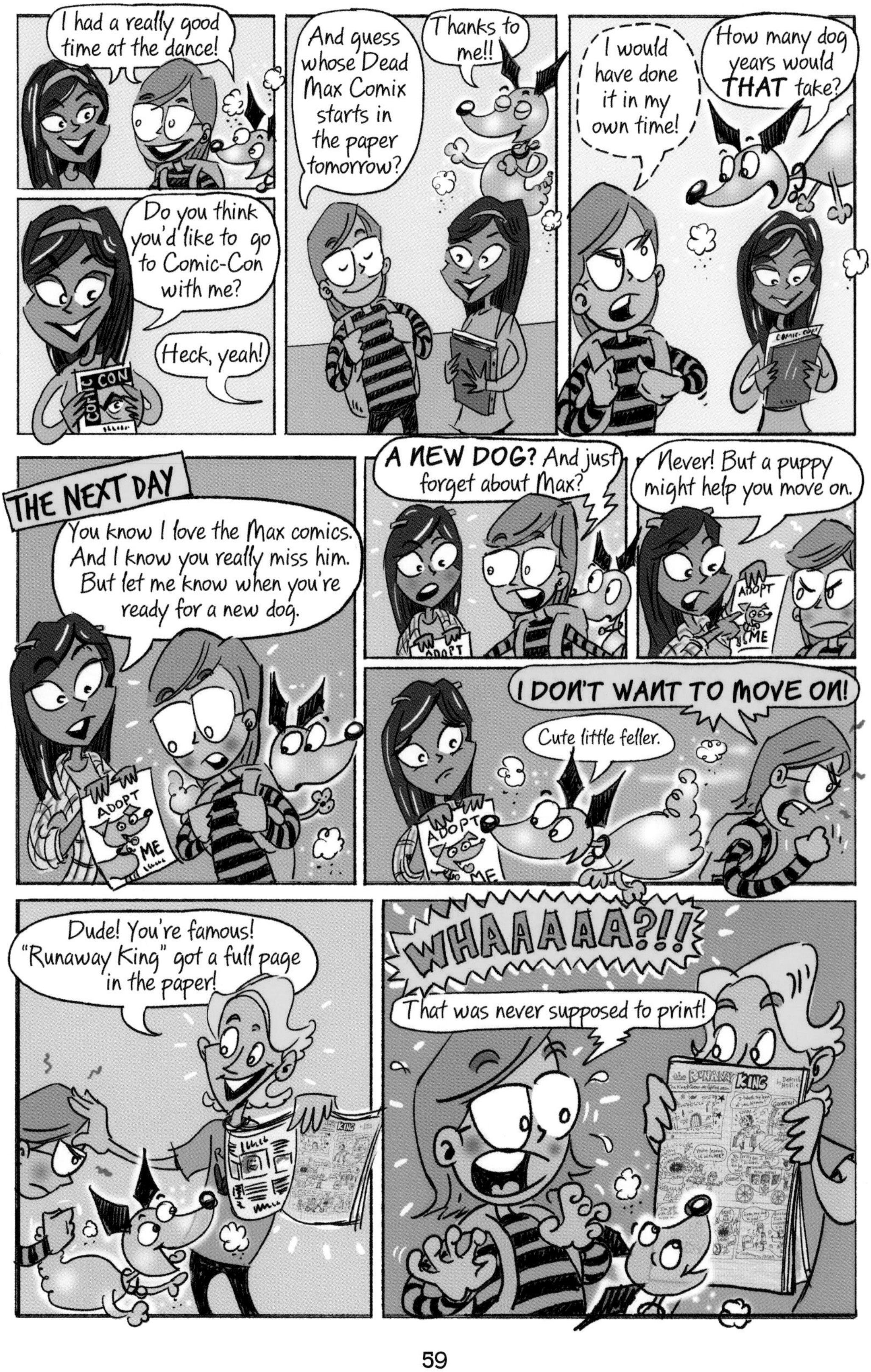
I had a really good time at the dance!
Do you think you'd like to go to Comic-Con with me?
Heck, yeah!
And guess whose Dead Max Comix starts in the paper tomorrow?
Thanks to me!!
I would have done it in my own time!
How many dog years would THAT take?
THE NEXT DAY
You know I love the Max comics. And I know you really miss him. But let me know when you're ready for a new dog.
ADOPT ME
A NEW DOG? And just forget about Max?
Never! But a puppy might help you move on.
I DON'T WANT TO MOVE ON!
Cute little feller.
Dude! You're famous! "Runaway King" got a full page in the paper!
WHAAAAAA?!!
That was never supposed to print!

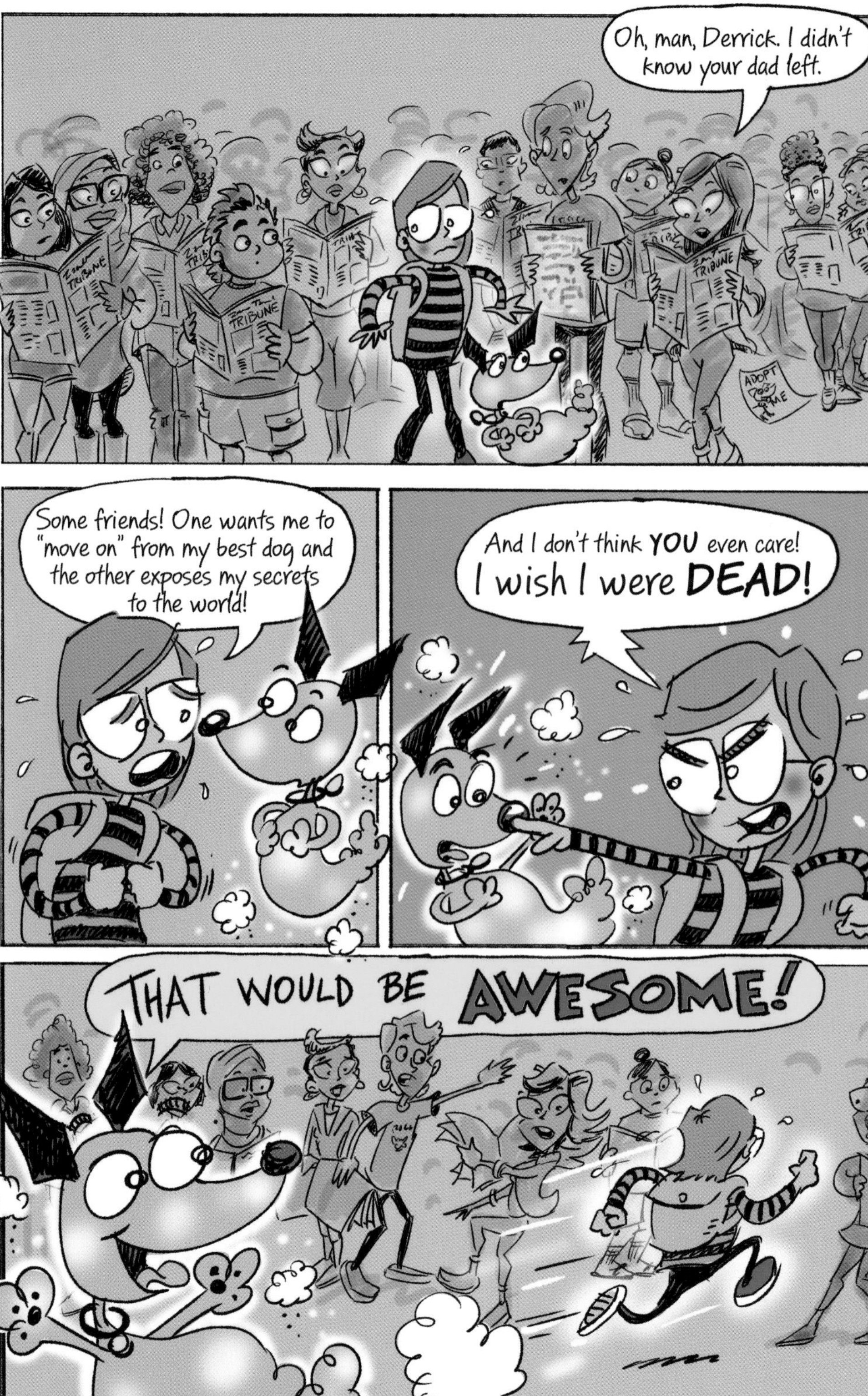
Oh, man, Derrick. I didn't know your dad left.
TRIBUNE
ADOPT ME
Some friends! One wants me to "move on" from my best dog and the other exposes my secrets to the world!
And I don't think **YOU** even care!
I wish I were **DEAD!**
THAT WOULD BE AWESOME!

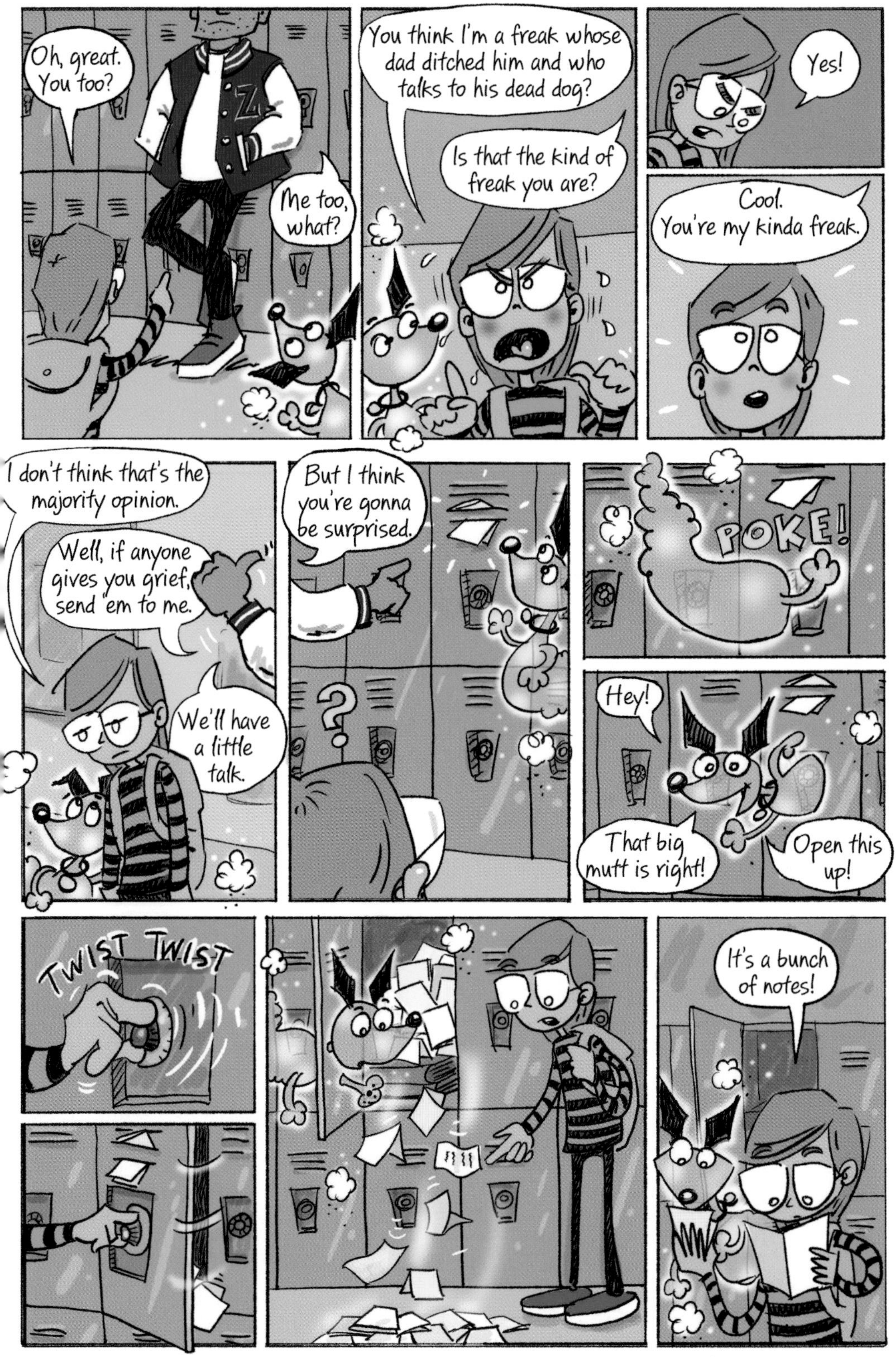
Oh, great. You too?
Me too, what?
You think I'm a freak whose dad ditched him and who talks to his dead dog?
Is that the kind of freak you are?
Yes!
Cool. You're my kinda freak.
I don't think that's the majority opinion.
Well, if anyone gives you grief, send 'em to me.
We'll have a little talk.
But I think you're gonna be surprised.
?
POKE!
Hey!
That big mutt is right!
Open this up!
TWIST TWIST
It's a bunch of notes!

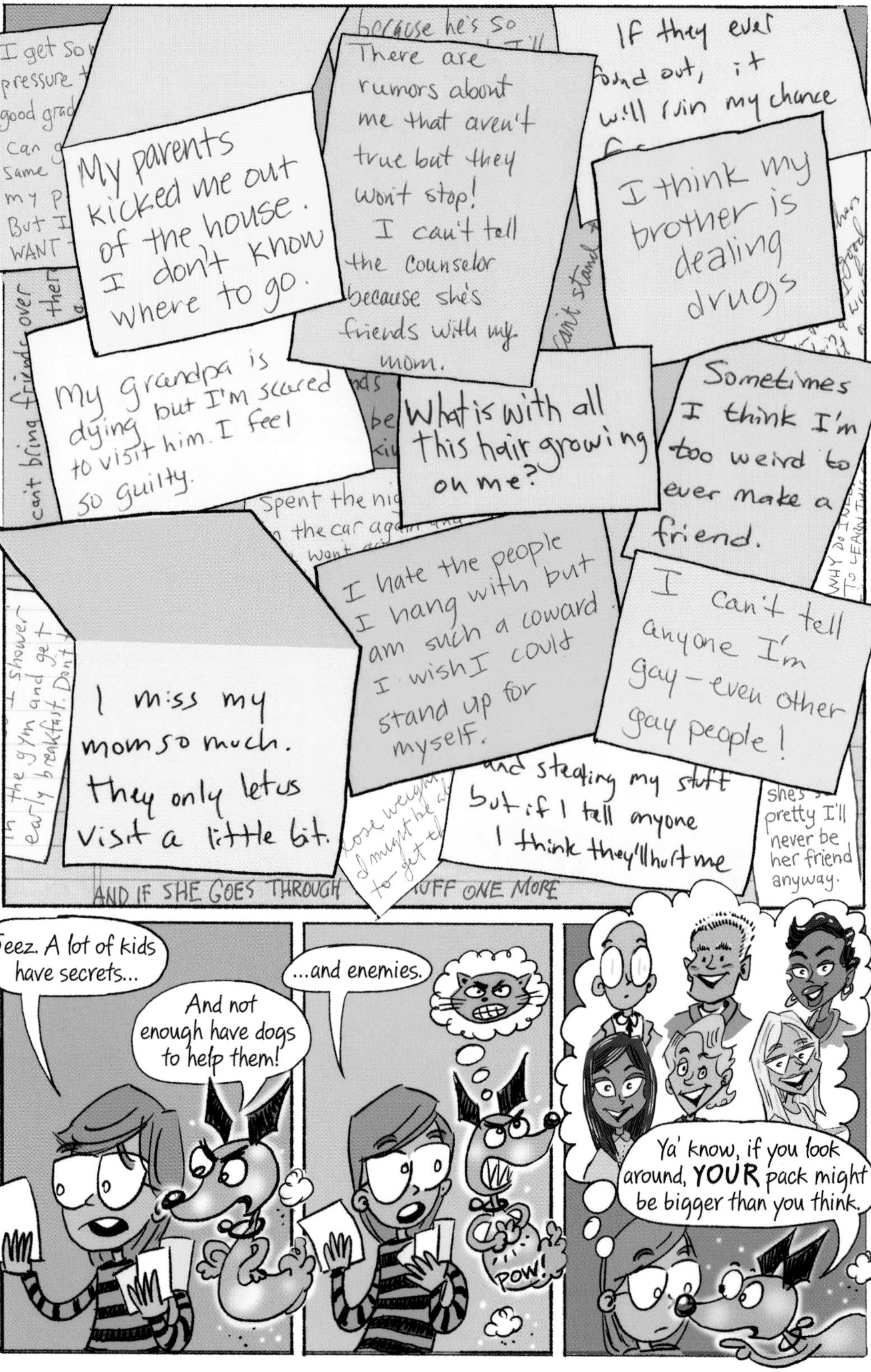

If they ever found out, it will ruin my chance
I get so much pressure to get good grades
My parents kicked me out of the house. I don't know where to go.
There are rumors about me that aren't true but they won't stop! I can't tell the counselor because she's friends with my mom.
I think my brother is dealing drugs
My grandpa is dying but I'm scared to visit him. I feel so guilty.
What is with all this hair growing on me?
Sometimes I think I'm too weird to ever make a friend.
Spent the night in the car again
I hate the people I hang with but am such a coward. I wish I could stand up for myself.
I can't tell anyone I'm gay—even other gay people!
I miss my mom so much. They only let us visit a little bit.
and stealing my stuff but if I tell anyone I think they'll hurt me
she's so pretty I'll never be her friend anyway.
AND IF SHE GOES THROUGH
UFF ONE MORE
Jeez. A lot of kids have secrets...
And not enough have dogs to help them!
...and enemies.
POW!
Ya' know, if you look around, YOUR pack might be bigger than you think.

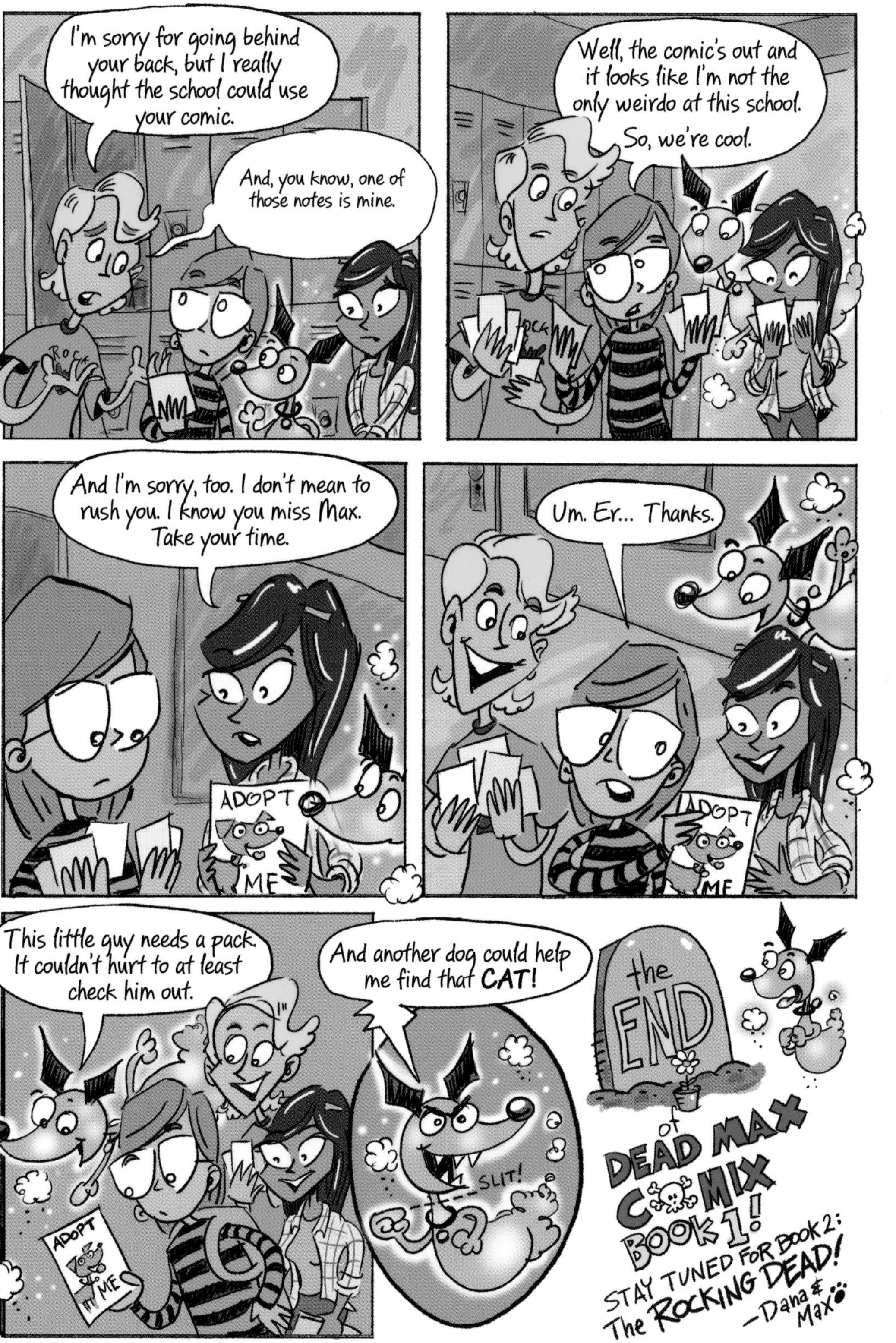
I'm sorry for going behind your back, but I really thought the school could use your comic.
And, you know, one of those notes is mine.
ROCK
Well, the comic's out and it looks like I'm not the only weirdo at this school.
So, we're cool.
ROCK
And I'm sorry, too. I don't mean to rush you. I know you miss Max. Take your time.
ADOPT ME
Um. Er... Thanks.
ADOPT ME
This little guy needs a pack. It couldn't hurt to at least check him out.
ADOPT ME
And another dog could help me find that CAT!
SLIT!
the END of DEAD MAX COMIX BOOK 1!
STAY TUNED FOR BOOK 2: The ROCKING DEAD!
—Dana & Max

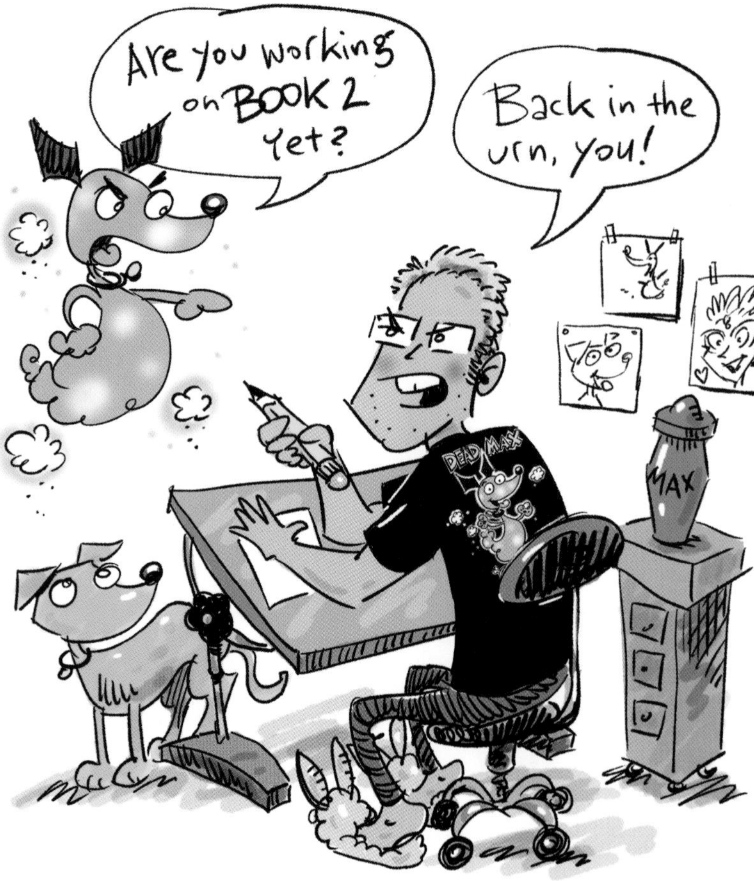
Are you working on BOOK 2 yet?
Back in the urn, you!
DEAD MAX
MAX

Dana Sullivan grew up in Southern California drawing on every piece of paper he could find, especially his math homework. He kept at it until somebody finally published his books. He's written and illustrated a bunch—you can look 'em up if you don't believe it. He even teaches picture book and graphic novel classes.

Dana now lives near Seattle with his sweet wife, Vicki, and their two dogs: Bennie, who barks at the door a lot and takes Dana for a hike every day, and Max, who mostly stays in his urn. Dana's favorite color is dog and his favorite vegetable is peanut butter. See Dana's stuff, write him silly notes and send him even sillier drawings at www.danajsullivan.com.

Max and Dana know what it's like to be a kid going through stuff they don't want to share.
But know this: **YOU ARE NOT ALONE**! Here are two excellent confidential resources:

Crisis Text Line: 741741 (USA) or 686868 (Canada) to connect with an online volunteer
National Suicide Prevention Lifeline: 1-800-273-TALK (8255) suicidepreventionlifeline.org

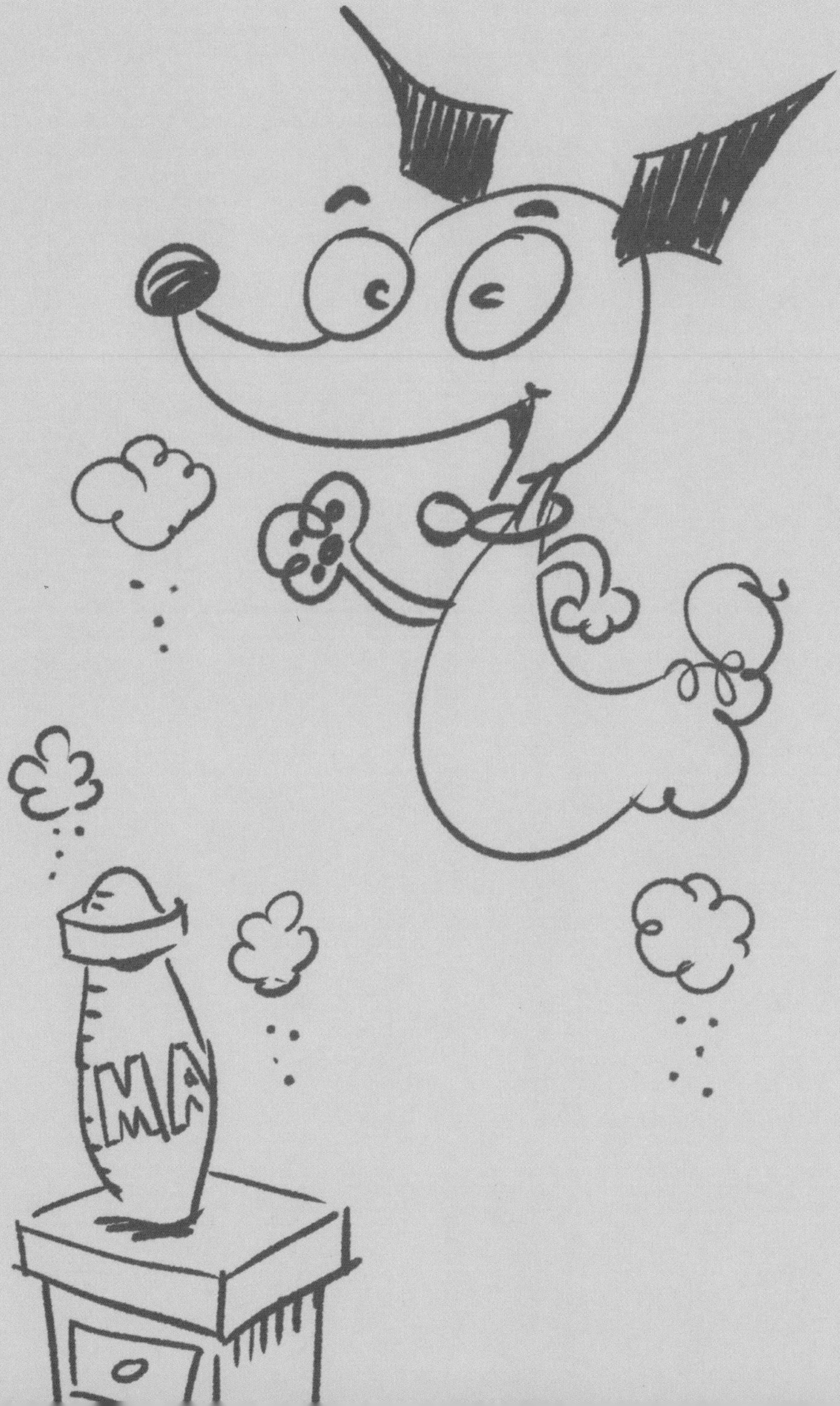
MA

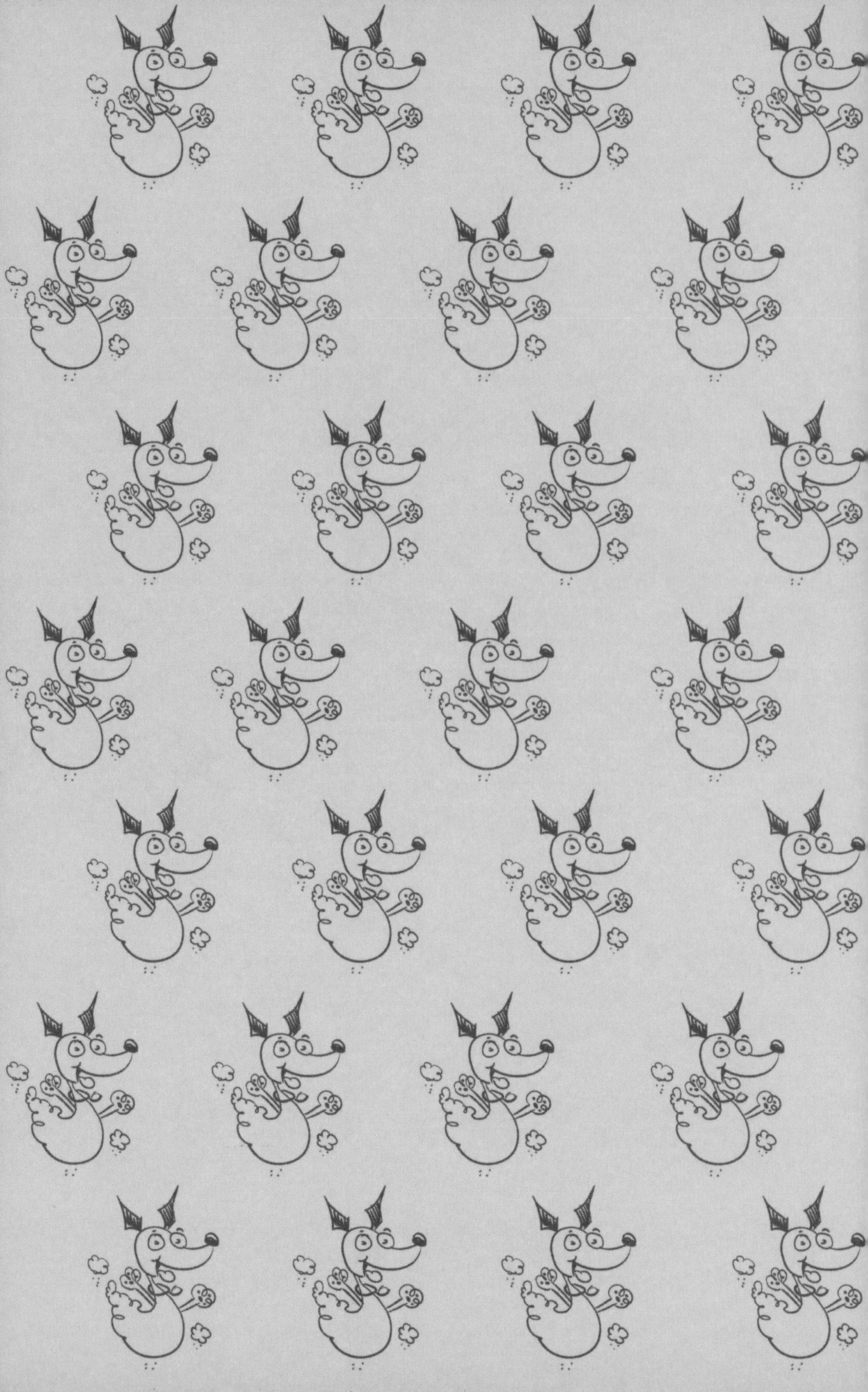